Conrad's War

Conrad's War

ANDREW DAVIES

CROWN PUBLISHERS, INC.
NEW YORK

Published in the United States in 1980.
Copyright © 1978 by Andrew Davies.
Published in Great Britain in 1978.

Manufactured in the United States of America

10   9   8   7   6   5   4   3   2   1

The text of this book is set in 12 point Baskerville.

Library of Congress Cataloging in Publication Data
Davies, Andrew.   Conrad's war.   Summary: Currently fascinated with wars,
army, killing, and guns, Conrad becomes convinced that through dreams or time warp
he is experiencing action in a past war. [1.War—Fiction] I.Title.
PZ7.D2837Co   1980   [Fic]   79-28289   ISBN 0-517-54007-X

To Bill Davies,
who supplied a lot of ideas
for this book

Contents

Prologue

Conrad got up in the dim light of dawn. They were all snoring. He went around the bedrooms looking at them. Snoring in their beds. Conrad was in charge.

He went downstairs and put a sheet of paper in his dad's typewriter. Conrad at the controls, he said to himself. He typed with two fingers. He typed so hard that some of the letters made holes in the paper. He typed:

DAD IS FAT

Then he went back to bed and read comics.

Bad Times
at Breakfast

Later that morning Conrad stamped upstairs with the mail, in a rage. Conrad was in a rage most of the time. He liked the feeling. He was pounding the stairs so hard he was jarring his knees, but he didn't care.

Four letters: Mr. and Mrs. J. D. Pike;
     J. Pike Esq.;
     Joe Pike;
     Mr. J. Pike.

Nothing for Conrad.

He rattled the doorknob of the bathroom.

His dad was in there.

His dad spent half his time in there.

His dad was supposed to be a writer, but as far as Conrad could see, he spent half his time in the bathroom, and the other half sitting around staring as if he'd just been knocked out.

"Dad!"

"DAD!!"

"What?"

"WHEN ARE YOU COMING OUT???"

"How should I know?"

"Four letters," said Conrad. "Three bills and a letter from the BBC to say your plays are no good."

Silence from the john. Conrad pushed the BBC one under the door.

"Says you're the worst writer in the world. Says don't send us any more plays till you can learn to write good ones."

More silence from the john.

"Are you *deaf?*

"DAD!"

Conrad's dad thought he was the best writer in the world. He was wrong. Conrad was the best writer in the world.

"Are you coming out or not?"

"In a minute."

Conrad went down to breakfast. He knew that when his dad came out, the smell would be lethal to boys.

At breakfast, Conrad talked about his invention. When he talked, he liked to rock his chair backward and forward, snap his fingers, scratch himself, get up and shuffle about, and twitch his shoulders up and down. He found that the best style for him. Other people tired of it quickly.

"What I want to do," he said, pushing his chair back and snapping the fingers of both hands, "and I suppose you are going to say it's too ambitious or it won't work, so there really isn't any point in telling you . . ."

He paused to crack his knuckle joints and inspect his dad. The great writer was still in his scruffy old dressing gown and smelled of warm bed. The bald top of his head, worn thin by the great brains, gleamed dully, and his beard was full of fluff. He was staring at the Corn Flakes box as if it was full of bad news. He was not in good shape. Perhaps he was unconscious. It was often hard to tell.

The only thing to do was to go on.

"The idea," said Conrad, scratching, "is to get the *training* wheels off Florence's bike because she *doesn't need them,* and they *never worked anyway;* and also to get the wheels off her old baby walker—she *doesn't use it,* she's *not a baby*—and to get some of that wood and hardboard off the top floor—don't tell me it's yours because I know that, but you *never get around to doing anything with it* . . ." Conrad suddenly found that he had to get up and walk around kicking the radiators. He always followed impulses of this kind. They helped him to get his thoughts clear. Like now.

"And the idea is to get all these things and make a sort of TANK."

Silence from the beard.

Conrad pushed his chair in and out and found out how far you could tip it backward with one finger before it fell over.

"Well," he said, twitching his shoulders, "I say a tank, but really it's more of an armored car or half-track, big enough for me to ride in. I could mount an air gun on it. I KNOW I HAVE NOT GOT ONE, AND I KNOW YOU WON'T LET ME GET ONE. I was just mentioning it in passing, as a possibility. Anyway, what do you think of it?"

He stood on the chair and inspected the bald head for clues to brain activity. If his dad had a glass head instead of a skin one, he thought, he would be able to see all those great rusty wheels turning, or more likely standing still, with cobwebs on their cogs.

"Dad! WHAT DO YOU THINK OF MY IDEA?"

His dad turned his head slowly and stared at him as if he'd never seen him before in his life.

"What?" said Conrad's dad.

Conrad gave a cry of fury. He felt the need to stand on the table and did so. Twitching and snapping, he told his dad the whole plan over again. A few things on the table fell over, and some slices of bread fell on the floor. The dog took them away to eat.

"*Now* tell me what you think of my plan," said Conrad. His dad looked around the room and after a while seemed to see Conrad.

"What are you doing up there?" he said.

"I don't know," said Conrad. "Anyway I asked first. What about this tank?"

His dad groaned. "I don't know anything about tanks," he said. "If you think you can make it, make it. If not, not."

"But will you *help* me with it?" said Conrad.

"No," said his dad. "I have to be frank. I don't think I will."

"YOU NEVER HELP ME WITH ANYTHING!" roared Conrad. "You have no SYMPATHY or GRATI-TUDE!" He was in a rage again. He glared at his dad's head for a few suspenseful moments, then leaped off the table, jarring his knees again, and went upstairs to work on the tank by himself.

Problems of an Inventor

The tank was not working out. Conrad went into his dad's room. Things were as usual for that time in the morning during the school holidays. Mom at work. Florence playing with her dolls and teddy bears; they were being sick again. Florence was very interested in sickness. And Conrad's dad was doing his push-ups. Conrad watched him.

Conrad's dad could do more push-ups than Conrad, but he had an unfair advantage, Conrad thought. His belly was so fat that it was still on the floor supporting him even when his arms were stretched out. Despite this he groaned a lot, and sometimes his face turned a frightening color.

Conrad lay down facing his dad, whose eyes were bulging blindly.

"How many have you done, Dad?" he said.

No reply from the great writer.

The great writer looked about to burst, or suddenly turn inside out.

"My tank is not working out," said Conrad.

Conrad had a very clear vision in his head about how the tank should be. Wood and hardboard and Florence's wheels; yes, all right; but somehow as well a great, throbbing metal juggernaut lurching deafeningly over bleak, bomb-scarred landscapes through black days and starless nights—dangerous, invincible, Conrad at the controls. The vision came and went. Conrad felt the beginnings of rage. The tank was not working out.

"*Why* won't you help me?" said Conrad. "Other people's dads help them. Paul Mitton's dad built him a go-cart."

With a great groan Conrad's dad fell flat on his belly and lay there gasping and sweating. He had done his twenty. The exercise seemed to have done him even more good than usual. His eyes closed. Was he dead? Why was he so useless?

"Why are you so useless, Dad?" said Conrad. "Why are you no good at making anything?"

After a moment his dad opened his eyes. "I am good at making things," he said.

"What things?"

"I make imaginary worlds. I imagine things, and people see and hear them."

For a moment, Conrad saw again the bleak bomb-scarred landscape lurching and dipping as he scanned through the observation slit. Then he remembered the useless pile of wood and hardboard and broken toys in his room.

"That's not making things, big head," he said bitterly. The bleary eyes seemed to focus on Conrad for the first time that day. The great writer studied his son for some moments.

"Give us a kiss," said Conrad's dad.

"Aargh! Not that!" howled Conrad, and cannoned out of the room to find Towzer.

Towzer was lying on his chair. Very warm, very furry, smelling extremely strongly of his rich old self. Conrad fell on his body, and Towzer stretched to accommodate him.

"My furry friend," said Conrad. "How are you, my furry brother?" Towzer yawned.

"Are you bored then, Towzer?" Conrad stuck his face right into the thick, furry pile. Then he kissed Towzer on the snout. Towzer sneezed in his face. Soon he would wake up, and they could have a blanket fight.

Conrad often wished he was a dog, a Towzer dog. Towzer did a few things very well, like eating, sleeping, escaping, blanket fighting, leg hugging, sneezing, and shouting. Things he did not do well—heeling, begging, Dying for His Country—he left alone entirely. He seemed to have no trouble at all knowing what he wanted to do, and you always knew just where you were with him, unlike some that Conrad could name not a million miles from this dog chair. Towzer was all right. Conrad laid his skinny body on Towzer's strong, stout chest and listened peacefully to his furry brother's quick heartbeats.

Here are some of the things that Conrad was keen on: Wars, Army, Killing, Guns, Towzer.

It was all right to be keen on Towzer, but he had arguments with his dad about the first four, and with his mom, when she was home. They would go like this:

CONRAD: I want to watch this war film on TV.
MOM: Well you can't. Sorry.
CONRAD: Why not?
MOM: Too violent.
CONRAD: But I *like* violence! Anyway, wars are *supposed* to be violent! Whoever heard of a war that wasn't violent? You know I like army things. Why are they all on so late at night? And anyway why couldn't I see *Electra Glide in Blue?* It looked great in the preview.
MOM: It was an X-rated film. You have to be eighteen.
CONRAD: *Why?*
MOM: Too much killing and blood in it.
CONRAD: But I *like* killing! I *like* blood! Just because you're not interested in killing and blood. It's not fair.
Silence from Conrad's mom.
CONRAD: Well, can I watch it or not?
CONRAD'S MOM: No.
Exit Conrad's mom.
CONRAD: You're just going because I'm winning. That's very rude. You've got no manners or consideration. Dad! DAD!!!
CONRAD'S DAD: What?
CONRAD: Why shouldn't I watch films with killing and blood in them?
DAD: Please don't stand in the marmalade.
CONRAD: Sorry. Anyway. Don't *you* like killing?

DAD: No, I hate it.

CONRAD: You must be crazy. I love it.

DAD: You don't really.

CONRAD: Don't tell me what I like.

DAD: I mean, you wouldn't like to kill someone yourself.

CONRAD: I would. I'd like to kill Wayne Morris. I'd like to blast him with a fifty-two millimeter shell gun.

DAD: You wouldn't really.

CONRAD: Well he shouldn't keep beating on me. I wouldn't really do it, no, don't worry. I know I'd have to go to a special school if I did.

DAD: A school for killer boys.

CONRAD: But I'd do it if I could get away with it.

DAD: Wouldn't you feel sorry for him?

A short pause.

CONRAD: Not really.

A long pause.

CONRAD: Dad! DAD! Can I watch this film or NOT?

They would go like that, more or less.

Conrad at the Controls

When he was small, Conrad had once seen something on the news on television. This lady had been crying about her baby. Her room was in a cellar, and there was water streaming down the walls, and the baby had always had a cough, and then it had died. It was the first time Conrad had realized that babies could die as well as old people who had just worn out. He had been very sad and frightened, and even now when he thought about it he felt a tight feeling in his chest and a weak, melting feeling between his legs and a strong urge to run upstairs to the bathroom.

That was dying. Of course that was sad. What his dad did not seem to realize with his great brain was that *killing* and *army* and *war* were quite different, not at all the same thing. Thinking about them made him feel strong and dangerous, not frightened and melting.

But yet, when he got those glimpses of Conrad at the controls—the great dark tank vibrating around him as he struggled to hold it on course, hurtling drunkenly down the sides of bomb craters, leaning dangerously on inclines, thundering along the featureless, flat, black plains at forty miles an hour, only a dark, jerking, changing oblong of the world visible through the slit—when he thought of that, sometimes he felt a shudder take him from inside and shake him.

By eleven in the morning Conrad had watched his television programs. He turned it off and listened to the moving sounds in the big house: the whirring of the wind down empty chimneys and in the cellar; a window banging in the big junk-and playroom on the top floor; the washing machine going into the spin cycle; the great writer's typewriter (very spasmodic as usual); Florence and her dopey friend:

"I hate school."

"So do I."

"I'd rather be at school than be sick though."

"I'd rather be at school than be sick too."

"I'd *much* rather be at school than be sick."

"So would I. *Much* rather."

Conrad rolled his eyes, gnashed his teeth, and delivered two lethal karate blows in the quiet, dusty air in his room. To think that people found *him* boring!

He stumped down the stairs and into the front room.

He stood still in the doorway.

His dad was sitting staring straight in front of him with his fingers on the keys of the typewriter. He looked as if he had just seen a ghost. Conrad could see the white nearly all the way around his eyes. Had he gone crazy? Would he ever recover? Perhaps he was going to be sick!

"Wake up, Dad!" shouted Conrad affably.

The bald head moved slightly, but the fat writer's eyes remained glassy. For all Conrad knew he might have had a knife sticking in his back.

"Some of my friends," said Conrad, man to man, "think you look nutty. They think you look like a mad, decrepit old tramp."

"Yes, yes," said his dad.

"I don't mind you looking mad, or even dead drunk," shouted Conrad, suddenly in a rage again. "But I do mind the way you never take any notice of anybody at all, in particular *me!*"

"Yes, yes," said the great writer again, like some bald and fuzzy-bearded mechanical doll.

Conrad had a cunning idea.

"So you're going to help me with the tank, eh?"

"No, sorry," said his dad. "Got this to do."

Foiled again.

Conrad felt a great urge to pick up the typewriter in both hands and smash it on his dad's shiny scalp—jolt those rusty wheels into a ticktock as fast and jerky as his own.

"Listen, Fuzz," he said between his teeth. "I am going to MAKE this tank tonight, and I am going to BLAST through this house in it, and HARD LUCK if you're in the way!"

When he had said this, he felt a lot clearer in his mind. The tank was going to be made; he didn't need to think about it any more. Somewhere out there in his imagination the tank was already grinding into life, revving up slowly, shaking off the dust and earth of thirty years' peace, getting ready for Conrad to blast through the house.

He watched Florence and her friend Celia. They were sitting side by side making dolls. It looked as if it might be quite good fun. Celia had gotten quite far with hers. Conrad's great technical brain could see at once how they were done. The little girls had drawn outlines of fat doll shapes on cloth and then cut double thicknesses. Celia had sewn hers together already and turned the whole thing inside out. She had stuffed it with scraps of cloth and wool. It had fat stumpy arms and legs and a great fat head with stuffing coming out of the top.

None of Conrad's friends could possibly see or hear, so he sat down. "That looks good," he said.

"You being sarcastic?" said Florence.

"No, and I bet you don't know what it even means," said Conrad.

"Do you really think they're good?"

"Yeah," said Conrad. "They're all right."

"Like to make one?" she said quickly in her little high voice. "I'll give you the stuff. I'll show you how."

"I don't make dolls."

How could she not see that he couldn't be her friend? It was impossible. He was her brother, that was what he was, and that was enough, for anyone.

But Celia's doll was all right. Just halfway between a lump of scrap material and a person. Before she had sewn the eyes on—that must have been only a few minutes ago—it had been nothing. A soft shape. Now it was something. It couldn't do anything to you, but you could do things to it. Celia felt his fascination with it. She wrapped it in a bit of cotton with only its face sticking out and cuddled it, her own bright face shining with excitement as she stared into Conrad's eyes.

These girls got on Conrad's nerves. Always trying to turn things into other things. He would like to strafe the doll with his Avro Lancaster, tie it to the dog's collar, knock it around till it lost its individuality.

"You're staring," said Florence. "You're staring like dad does."

"I am not, Fatty Florence," he shouted. "I can't spend all day looking at dolls. I have got to get the decals on the Avro Lancaster!"

As he stamped up the stairs she squealed after him: "I am not Fatty Florence, so you can just shut UP!" Then she started to cry. Not his fault. But he had better get in his room quick and become deaf and innocent. There was one pitch, one special frequency in Florence's shriek that would echo off the walls, make the radiators ring a sour echo, and even penetrate the leather skull of the great writer and bring him blundering up the stairs in a dazed rage, shouting in a random and frightening way into the faces of any visible children, making visiting children go pale and shake.

Conrad would always shout back, but he had to admit that he didn't like it. What was worst about it was that his dad *still* didn't see him; he *still* looked tranced or drunk. His dad called it the Red Mist. That was to make it seem funny and nice. But it was rage, that was what it was, too much like Conrad's own rages for comfort.

Sometimes Conrad thought that life in his house was like Dennis the Menace in the comic books. Dennis the Menace was funny when you were reading him. But living his life—

might that not be a bit frightening and worrying sometimes?

Too much thinking made Conrad's head feel hot. The thing to do was to concentrate on the Avro Lancaster.

Conrad had two Avro Lancasters. He had made them both himself, one from an Airfix kit, and the other out of Lego. It was the Airfix one he was looking at now—his latest and most expensive model. It crouched heavy and solid on the bedside table, complete except for its identification marks.

Lancaster, Lancaster—what a strong-sounding name. The most successful bomber of World War II. Thousands of them flying heavy and slow and straight through the bright flak patterns, bomb bays chock full of blockbusters, four huge propellers whirring, bristling with guns fore and aft.

Conrad's model had a pilot and a navigator. He had put them in; they sat neatly in their seats with gray, expressionless faces. The navigator had no legs. Conrad didn't know why. What were their names? Conrad didn't know. Florence had asked him that; she expected him to know everything. How did they feel? They must feel good in there. At the controls. He peered more closely. Then something strange happened. Conrad saw the pilot turn his head to the navigator. He seemed to be talking to him, even shouting at him. The navigator stared straight ahead and took no notice. The pilot began to wave his arms; he looked as if he might hit his colleague. What was the matter? What had gone wrong? Conrad forgot about the table, the room, the house. The plane was flying now. Wisps of cloud above wrinkled blue sea.

Great. He must be mad!

Of course, nothing had moved. It was a trick of the light, something to do with the Perspex and cement and the way Conrad had been moving his eyes. This Lanc would never fly. Two of the propellers had gotten clogged up with cement by mistake and turned only when twisted. The guns were jammed too. And the little men were just gray plastic. It would never fly.

Well, so what? It wasn't supposed to. It was a damn good model.

Better than Wayne Morris could do.

Better than the great writer could do.

The best model of the greatest model maker in the world.

The Night
of the Tank

That night Conrad lay in his bed twitching his feet and staring at the ceiling. It had not been a bad day. He had just about finished the Lancaster, and had even managed to tempt the great writer into a short game of soccer. His dad had wandered off absentmindedly in the middle of the game, and Conrad had found him later trying to play Florence's recorder in the bathroom, and had had to shout at him rather a lot about *manners* and *how would you like it if* and a few of the usual topics. Still, a short game of soccer had been had. Great saves by Conrad.

And when his mother had come back from work they

had taken Towzer blackberrying, which had been good but muddy.

Later he had fooled everybody with a plastic joke dog turd, which he had bought that afternoon. It was very realistic, and even made Conrad feel a little odd as he left it on the orange chair in the living room. Curled, slightly shiny, with a little pointed bit sticking up from the center of the coil. It had thoroughly disgusted everyone except Towzer, who liked it very much, and took it under the sofa and ate part of it.

He wasn't feeling at all tired.

That had been strange, that feeling he had had about the pilot and navigator of the Lancaster. And that feeling about his tank. Well, he hadn't made it.

A short time later he opened his eyes, feeling strong and determined. He got out of bed and started to assemble his tank. His hands were powerful and steady. He found that he could screw large screws into the sides without effort. He had made several plans on paper of what the tank was going to be like—much too ambitious, his dad had moaned. Much too ambitious, was it? In fact it might prove to be not ambitious enough. The parts were growing under his hands so quickly that he realized he would have to make the final assembly downstairs. The corrugated iron and sheet steel from the old oil tank (with only slight surprise he realized that he had moved on from wood and cardboard) was heavy to carry downstairs, but not too heavy for Conrad.

Quietly, because he knew his dad must be watching television, he crept through the hall, opened the door to the kitchen, took a chair to the back door, unbolted it, and went into the garage. He did not know what he was looking for. When he found it, then he would know. There was a dark bundle under a shelf. He pulled it out. An oxy-acetylene welding torch in full working order with all the accessories. He had never seen one before but that was what it had to be. You could weld a tank together with a thing like that. What was it doing there? Maybe his dad had once thought of being a welder instead of a writer.

Conrad went back into the house. Everything was all right. The television was blaring away—probably something with violence and killing. They never showed those when the people who could really appreciate them could watch. He lugged the huge metal panels through the kitchen, enjoying his new strength. His pajamas seemed to have expanded to fit his bulging muscles. Outside the breeze was agreeably cool on his bare ankles.

He put on the goggles. Everything felt solid, squared off, sure, certain. Not only did he know just where everything had to go, he knew he could get it done. Showers of sparks danced dangerously about the rickety old wooden garage, illuminating old tricycles, old magazines, abandoned do-it-himself projects of the twit writer. The tank took shape, its sides looming steep, ugly, and heavy above Conrad. He found he was having to climb the rough rusty flanks to reach the welding points on the turret. But he could do it! He could do it! Conrad, the one-boy powerhouse! The little tank in his head burned clear and bright and made certain and solid the monster growing in the garage.

And soon, amazingly soon, it was done. Conrad's Centurion. How long had it taken? He didn't know. Was he tired? He didn't even know that. He felt sweaty and solid, and his hands and pajamas were black and greasy. He felt very good indeed.

He came out of his workshop and stood in the cool night, staring up at the stars. The grass was cool and damp around his ankles. Conrad's garden wore its grass a bit longer than most other gardens on the street. It was good, looking at the stars and feeling his tank brooding mightily in the garage. He went into the house again, taking no precautions this time.

"Mom!

"*Mom!*

"MOM!!!"

No answer.

He went into the living room. His dad was looking at the television set as if he was trying to understand what it was.

"WHERE'S MOM?"

"Think she's at an evening class," said his dad, with unusual speed of reaction.

"Well," said Conrad, "I've BUILT the TANK."

"Good," said his dad. "Do you mind not standing in front of the television?"

"You don't understand!" said Conrad. "It's massive!"

"Yeah, yeah. Good. Let me watch this."

"You've got to see it!"

"What?"

Conrad felt the rage rising. "I'll blast through the house in it!" he roared, climbing onto the television. "I'll drive it right through the living room!" he threatened, leaping off. Towzer looked up wearily.

"Do it quietly then," said his dad, shuffling down in his chair so that he could see the screen between Conrad's striped and skinny legs.

"Right," said Conrad. "You've asked for it. I'll try."

He stormed out through the French window, but stopped outside the garage. Had he been getting carried away again? He'd probably turn the corner and see nothing but rusty old garden tools and junk, or worse, a rickety, ramshackle, loosely nailed contraption like a decrepit baby walker that would probably collapse as soon as the bum of the great model maker settled in the cockpit. He took a breath and stepped around.

It was there. A huge, black looming presence. Parts of it were gleaming dully, a greasy dark green. The flanks were scarred and pitted and rusty. That made it more real and powerful. It wasn't a new tank. It had been in the war already.

Conrad climbed up the side, his slippered feet slipping on the greasy caterpillar tracks, and swung himself into the cockpit. He felt nervous and light-headed. It was a long way up. A voice in his head said, Set the extrensors. He set them. He reached for the cold, round metal knob of the starter. Felt it solid in his hand. Then he pulled.

There was a frightening roar; and the tank trembled, shuddered, then steadied into a juddering throb that made Conrad's teeth rattle. Through the slit he saw the walls of the garage flopping gently outward onto the grass like the sides of a cardboard box. This tank was really something! This something was really a tank! How had he known how to start it? How did he know that the next thing was to put it into gear? He knew it, that's all.

The tank nosed gently forward. There was enormous power there, but Conrad knew he could control it. With one hand he eased back the turret hatch; it slid back as easily as the sunshine roof on Angus's dad's car, and he stood up to drive and felt the cool damp night air on his face and the V of his pajamas. He took the Centurion on a wide arc that brought it smoothly around the apple trees by the fence and on to a course heading straight for the

French windows of the living room. He paused.

The curtains were open and the room was a bright silhouette like a good color snapshot. Conrad could see his dad's shiny head as he sat slumped in his chair watching television. It all looked small and neat, like a scene in a doll's house. Conrad eased the Centurion up the steps. He could control it to a hairsbreadth. The front was an inch away from the window.

He eased it forward and let it touch the window. Through the controls he could actually feel the glass bend slightly inward. The window gave a slight groan, as if it knew what was coming. Conrad saw Towzer drop unhurriedly off his chair and pad out of the room. Then he eased forward again. There was an immensely satisfying, musical shattering sound, and the whole French window caved in and fell on the carpet. The Centurion nosed deafeningly on, crushing and splintering glass, wood, and bricks, and Conrad halted it when its nose touched the opposite wall.

It filled the living room almost completely. Conrad's head brushed the ceiling. The back of the tank still stuck out slightly where the rear wall had been. But it did not occupy the full width of the room. Far down on Conrad's right, the television set flickered pathetically on, its sound drowned completely by the mighty throbbing of the Centurion. And far down on Conrad's left, the great writer sprawled in his chair, looking at his son with deep respect.

"What about THAT, DAD??" shouted Conrad.

"Fantastic," said his dad. "I have to admit it."

He wasn't even craning his neck to see the TV around the edge of the tank. He wasn't staring blankly into space. He was giving Conrad his full and undivided attention. There was no doubt about it. Conrad had really impressed his dad at last.

A Strong Smell of Diesel

Conrad was awake. What was the matter? The room was all wrong. It was too light. He was on top of the covers and not in them. He could smell breakfast. What were they doing, cooking breakfast while he was still in bed? He was always the one who woke first. He felt overtaken, outwitted. He would have to show them all where they got off. He sat up so suddenly that he made himself dizzy.

The tank. The tank! Had it happened or not?

It might still be there in the living room. They might all be standing around it, staring blankly, perhaps with a man from the Fire Department. His dad might be saying, *"My* son Conrad the inventor drove it through the wall last night. He's like that, you know."

Some hopes! Still, he had to see. He sneaked downstairs, passing Florence's room where she lay still asleep with about forty or fifty teddy bears. The great writer was moaning to himself in the kitchen as he fried bacon. Conrad passed undetected into the living room, bracing himself for the amazing sight.

Nothing. Nothing at all. Unless you counted papers, books, and more rubbish strewn around by the grownups. The French window was not even cracked, not even crooked. It was a tremendous disappointment, but a relief, too, in a shameful sort of way. In the light of day he felt a bit frightened of the tank he had made. It seemed too big and loud for him now. Even for the great Conrad.

He walked upstairs. The useless cardboard tank would be there on his bedroom floor still, he supposed, mocking him with its flimsy uselessness. He would have to give it up. After all this, he would have to smash it up and forget it.

But it wasn't there. There was no sign of it at all. Just a few scraps and some hardboard dust. Had someone swiped it, or had it really transformed itself into that huge, shuddering metal monster? He bent down to look under the bed, just in case, and he noticed that the bottoms of his pajama trousers were still damp. With traces of grass clippings. And something else, dark and sticky, rich and powerful. He was ready to bet it was diesel oil.

He drew his curtains and looked out. He was looking for caterpillar tracks, and he saw none. But what he did see was nearly as good. His dad's garage had collapsed, and lay strewn pathetically about the garden like a heap of old cardboard. Something *had* happened, then. He flung himself onto his bed, dislodging six comics, a leaking battery and a few emergency cookies, and began to apply his brains to the problem.

The first thing had been the feeling about the tank; he'd had that off and on for weeks. That sense that he knew what it felt like to be inside a Centurion, Conrad at the controls, hurtling over the rough terrain—such a strong feeling, strong enough to make his muscles bulge. He should have realized that there was something special about it. Then there had been the feeling about the Lanc, that somehow it was flying, despite its legless navigator and jammed propellers. Then last night, when he had made the tank and driven it, the feeling had been the same, only stronger and surer, and now it had started to leave traces behind it. Real things: grass, diesel, a smashed garage.

Started to leave traces? Was there going to be any more of it, then? Yes, there was, he felt sure. Why didn't he feel frightened? He ought to have felt frightened. Boys were supposed to be frightened of Alien Powers taking them over. Well, he didn't. He didn't even feel as if he was being taken over, he felt as if he was taking over *it*, whatever it was. Whether it was a time warp or a reality loop, Conrad was at the controls. His brain began to hurt a bit, and he went down to see how his dad was coping with the day's bad news.

His dad was sitting with his head in his hands.

"I suppose you know your garage is smashed to bits," said Conrad as an opener. No reply.

"He does know, yes," said Conrad's mother. "I think we'd better leave him to cope with the disaster in his own way."

"Good thing he's too lazy to put his car away," said Conrad. He helped himself to the Corn Flakes.

The great writer took his face out of his hands and stared blankly at his son. Was he going to get the Red Mist? No; he put his face back again.

"I'll help you put it back up," said Conrad. "The thing is, you'll have to do it properly this time. You didn't follow all the instructions last time; half the bolts weren't in the right places, were they?"

"Don't torment him, Conrad," said his mother.

"I'm not tormenting him. I said I'd help him, didn't I? I'll help him put it up after school."

"Not today, not today," moaned the great writer. "I can't face it today."

"Why not get someone to do it for you properly?" said Conrad's mother.

"Maybe I will. Not today, though."

"Well, I've got to get moving," said Conrad's mother. She was always on the move, always late for something. "Don't let it get you down, Joe." Conrad's dad groaned. Conrad averted his eyes as she kissed the shiny skin that covered the great brains. Then she went out.

"Where's Florence?" said Conrad. "Has she had her breakfast?"

No reply.

"Are we late or what?" said Conrad.

Suddenly his dad took his head out of his hands and stared at him in a curiously alert way. Conrad felt quite alarmed.

"I had an extraordinary dream about you last night," said his dad. "I was watching television in the living room, on my own, then I looked up . . ." He stared at Conrad in a puzzled way.

"And I came in through the French windows in a Centurion tank!" said Conrad triumphantly. His dad stared at him.

"Sorry," he said. "Did I tell you first thing this morning?"

"No," said Conrad. "I know all about it because I did it. It was me in the tank, wasn't it?"

"In my dream," said his dad.

"It happened," said Conrad.

"This is very weird," said his dad. "We must be telepathizing. I haven't done that with anyone for years." He was really looking at Conrad with full attention, just as he had looked last night.

Conrad basked happily in the spotlight.

"This tank," said his dad, "was really gigantic. It filled the room."

"Well, a Centurion would, wouldn't it?" said Conrad. "I thought of crashing through into the dining room, but I stopped when it touched the wall."

"Yes, that's right," said his dad. "Can you remember what you said to me?"

"Oh, something like 'What about that, Dad?'"

"Yes, it was something like that. I could smell this tank," said his dad. "And the noise it made was deafening. I can't remember having a noisy, smelly dream before."

"It wasn't a dream," said Conrad. "It happened."

"How did it happen?" said his dad.

"I made it," said Conrad. "I made it in the garage . . ." He stopped and looked at his dad apprehensively.

"You couldn't have," said his dad slowly. "A tank like that would be too big for the garage."

"Just a little," said Conrad before he could stop himself.

"You smashed my garage," said the great writer, as if trying it out for sound. Why wasn't he angry?

"I didn't mean to, honest," said Conrad.

"You smashed my garage with an imaginary tank. Is that what you're trying to tell me?"

"It wasn't imaginary, it was real!" shouted Conrad. "I keep telling you!"

"How could it be real? Have some sense."

"Time warp! Reality loop! One of those things!" shouted Conrad, getting up and striding around. "Haven't you ever heard of time warps?"

"Vaguely," said his dad. "What are they?"

"Well, you don't think this is the only possible universe, do you?" said Conrad, walking around and snapping his fingers. "You don't have to think of time and space as just going along in a straight line. Yesterday is still here, if you wanted to get back into it. How do we know when all this is happening? Or where?"

Conrad was amazed at the power of his brain. For a moment he felt he had it all in place. His dad was in difficulties, though.

"Well," said his dad. "It's Monday morning, and we're sitting in the kitchen. Well, I am, and you're skidding about the room."

"Call yourself a great writer," said Conrad. "This kitchen might be anywhere, it might be hurtling through space. If we could get through the door fast enough, we could get out of space time. We might be anywhere."

"You mean," said his dad slowly, "if we went through the kitchen door, we might find ourselves on Mars in the twenty-fourth century."

"Why not?" said Conrad.

"Or," said his dad, "if we went in the living room, that tank might still be there."

"Much more likely," said Conrad.

His dad stared at him. "Doesn't all that sort of thing bother you?" he said.

"Why should it?" said Conrad. But it did, in a way—or rather, he felt that it should, but it didn't. Just now it exhilarated him.

"Where do you get all this stuff?" said his dad.

"Television!" said Conrad. "Comics! School! Everyone knows it, I'd have thought. Haven't you ever heard of relativity?"

"Television?"

"You just watch the wrong programs," said Conrad, kicking the water heater. "You can't expect to get anything about it in plays about nurses crying, or people carrying on about sex."

His dad stared at him. "You're being very perspicuous today," he said.

"I'm always perspicuous!" shouted Conrad. "All the time!" (What did perspicuous mean?) "It's just that you never listen to a word anybody else says!"

"Well, I'm listening now. You reckon there's a fair chance that tank will be back in the living room now?"

Conrad let his mind go blank for a moment. It didn't feel as if there was a tank in the living room. "I don't think it's there now," he said. "But it might be."

"Let's have a look," said his dad. This was amazing. The great writer looked quite excited and nervous. He got up and stood by the kitchen door as if he didn't like to go through without Conrad.

"Oh, come on," said Conrad. "I don't suppose it's there. Do you want me to hold your hand?"

"Heartless brute," said his dad, and together they went into the living room.

No tank.

Window intact.

But a powerful warm rich smell of diesel!

The great writer stared at his son. "Is this a trick?" he said.

"No," said Conrad. "It's just that the tank's very near. It's almost here."

"What do you mean, almost here?" said his dad.

"I don't know," said Conrad.

"You'd better go to school," said his dad. "You're ruining my thought processes. I'm supposed to be writing a play today."

"What about?" said Conrad.

"Oh, you know," said his dad. "Nurses crying and people kissing each other."

Conrad gave a snort. "You ought to write about this," he said.

School was a washout, as usual. In the morning he smashed through all the sums Parkin gave him in half an hour, but when he settled down to read his war books, she called him to the front of the room and gave him some more.

"You're a clever boy, Conrad," she said. "We've got to extend you. Don't you agree?" Conrad never spoke to teachers unless he had to. He didn't now. He looked at Parkin grimly, then went back to his seat and smashed through the rest of the sums. Extend him. They were out to rot his brain, so far as Conrad could see.

No one would play army at playtime. They were all playing soccer except Nigel Creamer. Conrad just hung around trying to ignore Creamer's feeble attempts to talk to him. No one would play army at lunchtime either. They were all playing soccer again. Conrad took his time over the bag lunch prepared personally for him by the greatest writer in the world. His dad was certainly not the greatest sandwich maker in the world. The liver sausage and banana seemed to have been getting together during the morning to create a new taste sensation, and Conrad didn't like it. He wished Towzer went to school. Towzer would appreciate liver sausage and banana sandwiches.

His drink was in a plastic container with a top that leaked, inside a soggy plastic bag, which also leaked. The leaks always started with a tiny hole, which gradually developed into a huge tear, until you couldn't call the bag a bag at all, it was just a sheet of plastic. When that point was reached, the great writer would grudgingly break out another bag.

That was how it would be with the tank world, of course, Conrad suddenly realized. It was a leak rather than a warp. The war was leaking slightly into his life through one or two tiny holes. But the holes would get bigger. They always did. Until you couldn't tell which was the inside and which was the outside of the bag.

The Briefing

Conrad was awake. Wide awake. Not dreaming. The
landing light was making its usual pattern of shadows
through his half-open door. The Airfix planes hung motionless on their threads from the ceiling. The Lanc was by
his bed, still waiting for its final coat of paint, next to a
German Tiger tank. Absolutely nothing out of the ordinary. And yet something had woken him up. He clenched
his fists and stretched his arms above his head. They felt
like his own arms, not charged and powerful as they had
been on the night of the Centurion. What was going to
happen, then? He had the odd feeling, the feeling that he
was beginning to call the leak feeling.

He listened carefully for sounds of war. Nothing. Not even a plane going over. Nothing except his dad snoring. When his dad slept on his back his breathing would get steadily louder until he woke himself up with a piglike snort. Then he would cough, mutter, shuffle, turn, and the whole process would start again. It drove Conrad's mother mad, but Conrad quite liked to listen to it on the rare occasions when he lay awake. He liked to predict the sequence of sounds, and pretend that he was in charge of the amplifier. Conrad at the controls.

He listened to the snore sequence for two cycles, then got out of bed. He hesitated before stepping onto the landing, but it was quiet as usual. Nothing to worry about. He tiptoed into his parents' bedroom, confident that he would find nothing out of the ordinary. He was right. His mother was curled up like a little girl, and his dad lay on his back with his mouth open wide. What a charming sight. What was the great writer dreaming about? Nurses and bare ladies, likely as not. Very boring.

Conrad went to look at Florence. He had a strange feeling as he crossed the threshold, but again there were no war leaks here. Florence slept on her back too, but she didn't snore. She had her arm around a Womble and a rabbit. She looked nice when she was asleep, he had to admit. Conrad usually hated the feeling of tenderness for Florence that sometimes sneaked up on him, but when he was the only one awake in the house he could cope with it. Poor little girl. She knew nothing about war and army. She was lucky to have a brother who could protect her.

Conrad realized that he was deliberately delaying going downstairs. That was where the leak would be, if there was a leak. He wasn't frightened, but he wished he could have been given that surge of strength and confidence he had felt on the night of the tank. Maybe he would not need it tonight. He stepped out onto the landing, and made himself go downstairs.

The stairs creaked in the usual places, and the floor in the hall felt cool and smooth under his bare feet. But he felt a buzzing in his ears as he approached the door to the living room. This is where the leak must be. He took a breath and opened the door.

He was in the school hall. It was packed. He must be late for assembly. He sat down quickly at the back, hoping that no one had noticed him. Mr. Harris was a tiny figure in the distance on his platform. It was years since Conrad had sat this far back. But was it Harris? He had let his moustache grow long, he had gotten fatter, and he was in a blue RAF uniform. He was pointing at a map with a long stick, and everyone was listening intently through the smoke.

Through the smoke?

Conrad noticed with mild surprise that half the kids were smoking cigarettes and pipes as they lolled on the hard chairs, and the smoke was pluming upward to the low, curved ceiling, and floating down toward the back of the hall where he sat. Smoking usually disgusted Conrad, but he found that he could stand it now. He leaned forward and listened to the headmaster's words.

"Nuremberg is an important industrial city with a population of three hundred and fifty thousand," said Harris, pointing at the map.

What was this? A mass geography lesson? And why was everyone so excited?

"Blimey, Nuremberg," muttered the man next to Conrad. "That's a long way down." Conrad looked at him. He was grinning and showing all his teeth, a frightened-dog grin that Conrad had seen on the faces of boys waiting outside the headmaster's office. "Hope you had a good leave, Conrad," said the man. Conrad nodded impatiently and tried to concentrate on what Harris was saying. He scratched his thigh; the heavy blue serge was hot and itchy.

"That's only a bit smaller than Leeds, so you shouldn't have too much trouble finding your way to it." There was a bit of polite laughter. Conrad's grandmother lived in Leeds.

"This is a maximum operation, men. We're going to knock it off the map. The main targets are the M.A.N. tank factory, the Mueller works, and Siemens. After that, between 0105 hours and 0122 hours, you'll be saturating the whole target area with high explosives and incendiaries. Good luck."

Harris sat down and another man took his place. Conrad didn't recognize him. All around Conrad people were taking out notebooks and pencils. Conrad found one in his uniform and found himself scribbling notes in a handwriting smaller and neater than his usual large, rounded scrawl.

"Number five group." That was Conrad, he knew. "Rendezvous over the North Sea at 51°50′ north and 2°30′ east and then fly southeastward. Then turn port and fly east. Finally turn and fly southeastward straight on to Nuremberg."

Conrad stared at the figures covering his notebook like a bit of new math in a foreign language, and suddenly knowledge flooded his brain as strength had flooded his muscles on the night of the Centurion.

It was too simple. They were advertising their attack on Nuremberg as clearly as if they'd put it in the paper.

Harris must have intended some sort of double bluff by taking the direct route, but he was putting them into the most heavily defended flak and night-fighter zones in Europe. Harris was mad.

Conrad found himself on his feet and heard his voice. "I want to ask a question, sir."

Hundreds of heads turned and stared at him through the smoke.

"Make it a quick one, Pike," said the thin man at the front. How did he know Conrad's name?

"Well," said Conrad. "Why aren't we making a feint attack? Why aren't we doglegging?"

"Bomber Command has calculated that the Germans will be expecting feint attacks. A direct run down to Nuremberg with a following wind of seventy to eighty miles an hour will take them completely by surprise. We should be right through their defenses before they wake up to it."

"You must be crazy," said Conrad. "They'll have plenty of time to wake up to it. What about all those Messerschmitts, eh? What do you think they're going to be doing, eh? They'll just be using us for target practice, that's what they'll be doing."

All over the hall Conrad could hear the hardened combat veterans muttering to each other in approval of his brilliant analysis of the situation. The thin man was starting to look cross, as well he might. People often started to look cross when Conrad argued with them.

"The weather people have promised us heavy cloud cover for the first half of the journey," said the thin man.

"Ha ha!" said Conrad sarcastically. "Heavy cloud cover and a seventy-mile-an-hour following wind, eh? Not going to be many clouds with all that wind, are there? Going to blow them all away, isn't it? I mean, which are we going to have, clouds or wind?" The thin man fiddled with his moustache.

"Got you there, haven't I?" shouted Conrad.

"Conrad's got you there," shouted the veterans.

The thin man looked uneasy. "I didn't say it was going to be a milk run," he said.

"You're telling us it's not," said Conrad. This was easier than arguing with his dad, even. He felt enormously clever and sarcastic.

"Bet you're not going, anyway, Wiseguy," he said, in his most scornful tone, and the veterans roared with laughter.

Harris got to his feet, looking very red in the face. "Right, men, that's enough," he said. "The briefing's over. Back to your quarters and wait for takeoff. And good luck."

"We'll need it!" shouted Conrad.

Well. That had told them. And serve them right too. What a nerve. Bringing him back from a forty-eight-hour leave and then sending him off on a long-range bombing mission with the craziest flight plan he'd ever heard of. Why hadn't they consulted him about the planning? Conrad could have worked out something fantastic. He should be the one in charge of Bomber Command, not Harris.

The men were coming out now. At least *they* appreciated Conrad at his proper worth. A lot of them patted him on the shoulder as they went past, saying things like "Well done mate," and "Good luck, Conrad."

Some of them looked very pale and tense. There was one, who reminded Conrad of Nigel Creamer, who was shaking so much he dropped his pipe just as he passed Conrad. The pipe shattered into little bits, and the man who looked like Creamer just stood there staring down at the bits and shaking. He looked as if he was going to cry. Somebody tried to pull him along, but he just stood there shaking.

Conrad stared at him. He *was* Nigel Creamer, only older. He had cut himself shaving, and he had a little bit of toilet paper on his chin.

His lips started to move, but no sound came out. Then he started to talk.

"I'm not going, I'm not going anymore, I can't go, it's not fair anyway, they know I've got asthma." The sound died away, but the lips kept moving. Conrad turned away in disgust. Of course he had to go. They all had to go. Asthma was no excuse. Everybody had to go. Conrad had to go.

Suddenly he felt chilly as he realized what that meant. It had felt good, being sarcastic and winning the argument with Bomber Command, but now it was over, and it was just like he said: Conrad had to go and they didn't. The thin man had probably agreed completely with Conrad about the crazy flight plan. He had just been trying to cheer them all up before they got in their planes to be shot at by the German night fighters. He had played at war for years, and now he was going to be in it.

Conrad was one of the last to leave the briefing room. Just time to go back to his quarters, loll around on his cot for a bit, maybe write a letter to his mom and dad—no details of what he was going to do, of course. Security. As he went through the door he felt strange; suddenly he couldn't remember the way back to his quarters.

He closed the door behind him and found that he was standing in the hall of his own house again. He was in bare feet. His RAF uniform had gone. He was in his own pajamas. He wasn't a pilot. He was a boy. Or was he? The leaks were beginning to get bigger. He was back inside himself now, but what would it be like next time? Maybe next time he would have to stay in the war, and there might be no way of getting back to his own house and his own bed and his own mom and dad and sister and Towzer.

He had a sudden urge to run upstairs and get in bed with his mom and dad and tell them about it and tell them to make it all go away and make everything safe and cozy. They would let him in all right, but he didn't think they'd be able to stop the leaks. Anyway, they would think it was all silly, they would think he was a little boy having nightmares. Conrad couldn't stand that. He was going to have to do it all on his own.

He stood at the bottom of the stairs and felt the courage draining out of him. It wasn't fair. He wasn't big enough for this adventure. He had to have someone with him.

Towzer! Towzer would do. Towzer wouldn't laugh at him, or tell people about it, or put it in some stupid play. He went into the kitchen and Towzer got out of his box immediately, as if he knew something was going on. He wagged his tail and sniffed all over Conrad's pajama bottoms. Conrad got him by the collar and lugged him upstairs to his room and shut the door. He tried to get Towzer to get into bed with him, but Towzer was puzzled by this break in routine and wouldn't lie down. He trotted back and forth, whining softly. It was irritating in a way, but it was good to have him there.

After thoroughly investigating the possibilities of Conrad's room, and checking for forgotten cookies, M&M's, and escape routes, Towzer let out a long, exasperated sigh and flopped down to sleep by Conrad's bed. Conrad lay awake, one hand on the Lancaster, one hand on his radio, waiting for whatever was going to come.

The Nuremberg Raid

The war was extremely cold, dark, uncomfortable, and bumpy, and it was making Conrad feel sick. This was one thing those stupid war comics left out entirely, he thought to himself as he clung to the controls of the great clumsy bomber as it thundered through the night. There were drafts everywhere; every piece of metal he touched was so freezingly cold he was afraid his skin would come off on it. Even though his leather flying jacket came up to his ears, and his flying boots almost up to his knees, he was teeth-rattling cold. It was worse than soccer in the January sleet with Mr. Hopkins.

"I thought airplanes were supposed to fly straight and

steady," he shouted to his navigator over the howl of the engines. "That's what they look like from down below. This thing is like a Donkey Derby." Conrad was not exaggerating. The plane seemed to proceed in a series of lurches, then suddenly drop what seemed the height of a house, lurch again, and only a heavy dose of throttle would get it to stagger along again.

"I said it's like a Donkey Derby," he shouted again. The navigator made no reply. Strong, silent type. Conrad sneaked a look at him as he sat there like a plastic dummy staring straight in front of him as if he'd just been knocked out. "You know," said Conrad, "you remind me of my dad, you do." Silence from the navigator. "You remind me *very strongly indeed* of my dad," said Conrad. The navigator was not provoked.

Conrad peered into the darkness, a great aviator concentrating on his task. They were supposed to be flying in close formation, which was (a) safer, (b) more devastating in attack, (c) looked smart on the photos. Just like all the school getting up and sitting down at the same moment instead of all higgledy-piggledy, the way they liked to do it. The only trouble was that Conrad didn't know whether he was flying in close formation or not because it was too dark to see any other planes. He had a prescribed height to keep to, but with all this lurching about it was quite likely that he'd drop on someone's head at any moment, or vice versa. Or run into the back of someone, or have someone run into the back of him. On the whole Conrad hoped that he was not flying in close formation, and that there were no planes within miles. Why didn't the books mention how difficult it was to see through the dark? When he got back he would certainly have something to say to Harris about it.

"Harris!" he would shout. "You have no sympathy or consideration!"

Harris would shuffle and mutter and go red.

"Like to see you fly one of your Lancasters in the dark and the cold," he'd say. "Anyway you'd be too *fat* to get into the *cockpit!*"

Harris would cringe and apologize and promise to do better next time.

"Not good enough!" Conrad would shout. Yes, he'd certainly have a good time telling Harris off when he got back. He'd tell him about the navigator, too.

"Worse than sitting next to Nigel Creamer!" he'd say. "Just sat there like a dummy all the time! I've seen better navigators in Airfix kits!"

The Lancaster lurched again, and the navigator slipped sideways.

"What's the matter with you then?" said Conrad. "Gone to sleep? You're supposed to be navigating this plane, can't do everything myself, can I?"

The navigator didn't answer. He was leaning over at a funny angle. For a second Conrad thought he might have been shot. Then he took a close look at his navigator. The man's face was gray and expressionless. Somewhere Conrad had seen that face before. A dummy in a store window? He gave the man a shove. He felt light and hollow and he rattled. Funny sort of navigator.

"Hey, Harris," he'd say. "You've given me a dud navigator. He rattles."

Conrad looked again. The navigator was in worse shape than he thought. Not only was he hollow and did he rattle, but his legs only went down to the knee. This was definitely not good enough for combat air crew. Then

Conrad realized what had happened. His navigator had come out of an Airfix kit. Well, a plastic navigator was no good. He gave the gray, expressionless gentleman a good kick to relieve his feelings and the hollow man shot out of his seat and tumbled over and over toward the dark cavern at the back of the plane.

"Hey," said a strangely familiar voice. "Steady there, Conrad. You're disturbing my train of thought. I was trying to do a bit of Yoga meditation back here."

Oh, no. It couldn't be true. The rear gunner was his dad. Conrad was encumbered not only with a useless, hollow, plastic navigator but a dozy writer of soppy plays to man the guns and shoot the night fighters out of the sky. Shoot the night fighters? His dad couldn't even hit his pop posters at six feet with a set of darts. What sort of operation was this going to be, Conrad asked himself. Good thing somebody knew what was going on, anyway. Conrad was going to have to run the whole show himself. As usual.

"It's not *time* for Yoga breathing!" he shouted. "You're supposed to be looking out for Messerschmitts."

"What do they look like?" called the great writer.

"They've got twin engines. Anything with twin engines is one of theirs." Imagine not knowing what a Messerschmitt looked like.

"What do I do when I see one?" shouted the great writer after a typically long pause.

"Blast it out of the sky!" What did he think you did with Messerschmitts? Ask them over for a drink? Another long pause. Doubtless the rusty brains were turning in the rear turret.

"But I can't stand violence."

"Well you're going to have to get some in, aren't you?" shouted Flying Officer Conrad Pike. "We all have to do things we don't like doing. I have to go to school and have my brain rotted in the classroom and play soccer in the sleet till I get pneumonia. The least you could do is blast a few Messerschmitts out of the sky!"

"Well, I'm afraid I can't see anything, Conrad," said his dad in a suitably humble voice.

"All right," said Conrad. "Just keep a look out and don't go into any of your trances."

Conrad couldn't see anything either. They had been flying through thick cloud all the way. The Weather Bureau had been dead right. They had said there would either be ten-tenths cloud cover, or alternatively a clear sky and a following wind. They had to be right one way or the other. Seemed like a nice easy job, doing weather forecasts. They couldn't give you a forecast for a bombing raid any more than they could tell you whether it would rain enough to get you out of soccer. Really brilliant.

But Conrad had to admit, it had been a picnic so far. A milk run. They might have been totally alone in the sky, no other plane in the universe, no ground below, no sky above. Just Conrad and his dad and the plastic navigator, skidding and lurching through cloudy blackness in the huge, roaring, drafty, cavernous Lanc with its load of blockbusters for Nuremberg.

The plane gave another lurch. A big one. Conrad checked his dials. One of the port engines was feathering. It would run fast, then hesitate for a split second, then feather around slowly, then pick up again. As if it was catching on something that was clogging it. Conrad felt a nasty cold feeling creep up his legs into his stomach. Something clogging it? Something, maybe, like polyurethane cement? If the navigator was made of hollow plastic, and the port engine was feathering, could it be that the Lanc he was flying was some sort of full-sized version of the less than perfect Airfix model he slept with every night? Conrad fervently hoped not. As a model kit it passed muster all right, but as a combat aircraft—well, he wished he'd spent a bit more time on some of the details. He had rather a nasty, apprehensive feeling about the bomb bays. They had been one of the trickiest parts of the kit, and in the end Conrad had gotten fed up with them and jammed them in anyhow, using more cement than was strictly desirable. They were probably jammed solid.

No. It couldn't be. That Lanc would never fly. It was just a coincidence. Conrad was in charge; the great aviator was at the controls; everything was responding perfectly except that port engine, and Conrad would pull them through. He forced the cold feeling down, out of his belly, down through his legs and out through his flying boots. He felt strong and capable and proud of himself. Conrad the invincible.

Something was touching his ear. Was it his fur collar? It tickled. He put his hand up and felt something damp and cold. Like a dog's nose. He jerked his head round.

"Towzer," he said. "What do you think you're doing here?"

Towzer wagged his tail. He seemed to be quite pleased to be on the Nuremberg raid, and sniffed all the instruments with keen interest. "Well, I don't know," said Conrad. "This is going to look pretty funny in the official histories of World War II."

Towzer looked as if he didn't give a damn. He sat in the navigator's seat and had a good scratch. Conrad reached in his pack for the emergency rations and gave Towzer and himself a piece of chocolate. Towzer swallowed his piece with the speed of light and barked for more. "No," said the aviator firmly. "This has got to last us to Nuremberg and back." Towzer flopped his heavy warm body across Conrad's legs and began to settle himself for sleep. Conrad tried to push him off, but Towzer exercised passive resistance. Conrad gave up and let him stay. It was against Air Force regulations to take a dog on a mission, and a violation of safety regulations to let him sleep on your legs, but Conrad felt prepared to take responsibility. Towzer's rich doggy smell began to take over the cockpit and make it snug and safe.

Suddenly the cloud cleared. Conrad stared through the windshield and saw the sky full of aircraft. They had all been there all the time. Up above on the port bow were the vapor trails of two Halifaxes, and over on the right, too close for comfort, was another Lanc. Conrad could even read the identification markings. Far above and ahead and all around the night sky unrolled like an enormous dark blue bedspread studded with stars. It was an amazing sight; hundreds and hundreds of heavy bombers in the dark night sky.

Not dark enough. Not dark enough for safety. They were into the second half of the Weather Bureau's brilliant forecast: clear skies and a following wind. Just what they didn't need, now they were over occupied territory. Now the German fighter pilots would be getting into their planes, the night fighters which were faster, more maneuverable, and had more powerful and longer-range guns than the lumbering Lancasters. In a few minutes, maybe less, they would be weaving in and out of the squadrons, picking out targets at their leisure. Conrad suddenly recalled the shooting booth at the fair. A long row of battered metal ducks flew with the speed and panache of a snail's funeral from left to right across a black background.

You lined your gun up, and waited for one to cross your sights. There was plenty of time to squeeze the trigger slowly. Even Conrad's dad had hit one or two. That's what they would look like to the Messerschmitts, Conrad thought. The ducks would clang over backward and disappear from view. He didn't want to clang over backward and disappear from view. He wasn't frightened yet, but he felt angry and cheated. Wars should be fair. It wasn't right for one side to be like the ducks and the other side like the customers.

"Plane coming up behind!" The voice came from the fat writer. So his dad had stayed awake.

"What sort of plane?"

"Four engines."

"Don't shoot!" yelled Conrad. The next second a huge dark shape passed right overhead and veered away to the right. A Halifax going out of control with smoke coming out of its port wing.

The night fighters had gotten up among them already. Conrad and Towzer scanned the sky from left to right. No Messerschmitts to be seen. But far off to the left the sky lit up as flames burst from another Halifax, and Conrad leaned over to see it spinning down through the flak, with tiny figures leaping out of the cockpit, the parachutes blossoming like puffballs.

"Log it," said Conrad to Towzer, just to see what he'd do, and Towzer gave a gruff low bark.

Bombers were going down all over the sky, a few running straight into the box barrage aimed at random from the ground, but most falling to the invisible night fighters. On a clear night, Conrad knew, the Messerschmitts would come from the left low down, fire for the port engines, and veer away at the last minute to avoid the flying debris. He'd be lucky to see one before he was hit. If the fat gunner got one in his sights it would probably be too late. Conrad flew steadily on. There was no point in trying to avoid the box barrage. You just had to put your nose down and go straight on. They had been lucky so far; they ought to be on target soon.

Suddenly Towzer started to yelp hysterically, as if he'd seen a cat in the garden. Conrad glimpsed something out of the corner of his eye and pulled the Lancaster into a steep dive to starboard. A black shape hurtled across their bows from right to left and Towzer flung himself against the window as if he thought he could take the Messerschmitt by the scruff of the neck and shake it. Conrad caught a glimpse of two startled faces. Then it was gone and a split second later he heard the sounds of their own machine gun.

"Missed it," came the apologetic voice of the great writer in the gun turret. Towzer growled and grumbled to himself and settled down in his seat.

In a German plane a white-faced German pilot turned to his white-faced German friend. *"Donner und blitzen! Ein hund in dem Lancaster!"* With shaky hands he returned to base for a medical checkup.

The sky was empty now, though Conrad could see flak ahead, hurtling up and exploding uselessly in the black emptiness. He had no idea where he was; dogs and plastic Airfix men were not to be relied on for accurate navigation. Still, he'd drop his blockbusters somewhere, and he hoped he was over Germany.

Then he saw the flares, falling in vivid cascades of dazzling red and swinging gently under their parachutes like Christmas trees on fire. They were beautiful. They were better than anything he'd seen on Guy Fawkes night, they were like dream fireworks. Towzer stretched his neck and looked down with mild interest. He had never been one for fireworks himself. But Conrad was thrilled to the marrow. Not just because of the fireworks. He knew that the flares meant something. They were over target! Somehow he had piloted the cranky old Lanc all the way to Nuremberg. There was something he had to say, and just as he was wondering what it was he heard his own voice, crisp and curt like the pilots in the movies. "Bombs away!"

"Eh?" said the voice from the back.

"Bombs away, I said!"

"What am I supposed to do, then?"

"Can you see the drift handle on the bombsight?"

"Um . . . ummm . . . oh yes, there's some sort of handle here, Conrad."

"Push it forward!"

"Can I go back to my turret now?"

"NO!" yelled Conrad. "Slap down the selector switches!"

"How do I know what a selector switch is?" came the mournful voice.

Had there ever been such a dozy bomb aimer? They'd be back over England before they dropped their blockbusters.

"Slap down all the switches you can see then!"

"Switches all slapped down, sir!"

There was a long pause. Then the great writer said, "I'm feeling a bit sick, Conrad. Can I go back to my little turret thing?"

"No!" screeched Conrad. Why hadn't the doors opened? What had gone wrong? Those bombs should be plummeting down now. It wasn't fair. But deep inside he knew what was wrong. Too much glue again.

"You're going to have to jump up and down on the doors," he said.

"You must be joking, Conrad."

"Jump!"

"But I'm not an active man, Conrad."

"Jump! Those bombs are fused now; do you want them to go off in the plane?"

"No, Conrad."

"Then shut up and jump."

The fat bomb aimer, shortsighted rear gunner, and self-styled greatest writer in the world shut up and jumped.

"Nothing's happened, Conrad!"

"Jump again!"

The plane vibrated to the repeated clanging as the fat writer bounced on the bomb doors, puffing and wheezing. BONG *wheeze,* Bong *wheeze,* BONG BONG, cough cough, cough *wheeze* bong, BONG BONG!

There was a sudden rush of air, a shrill squeal, the red light went on, and a great surge of power as the Lancaster, free of its load of bombs, leaped forward joyfully. Towzer yelped and whined and jumped onto Conrad's knees.

They had done it! They had bombed Nuremberg!

"Conrad!"

"What now?"

"I'm afraid I've gotten stuck, Conrad!"

Conrad turned.

The great writer was wedged in the bomb bay with his legs dangling in the slipstream. Somewhere down below his boots were on their way down to enemy territory.

Conrad gnashed his teeth. "Can't you do *any*thing right?"

"I'm sorry, Conrad. You know war's not really my thing. Er . . . do you think you could get me out?"

Conrad wedged the controls and handed them over to Towzer, who sat in the pilot's seat staring ahead with a pleasing air of grim concentration. Back in the belly of the plane the plastic navigator was whirling around in the gale like a drunken gymnast.

It was a tricky situation, but Conrad felt capable of anything now. He held onto the guard rail to avoid being sucked out himself, and felt the mighty power surge into his muscles as it had done on the night of the tank. He grabbed his dad's arm and pulled.

"We'll never make it, Conrad. Oh dear, this is terrible."

"Push with your other hand," snapped the mighty aviator. "You know, you should be glad you're so greedy. You're just slightly fatter around the waist than a block-buster."

"This is no time for personal remarks," said his dad.

Conrad shut his eyes and heaved, and with a slow, sucking noise the great writer came out of the bomb bay and whirled around the plane with the plastic navigator like a couple of mad Apache dancers. Conrad pulled the lever twice, the bomb doors creaked shut, and the mad Apache dancers subsided and rolled gently to and fro on the floor of the plane. Conrad's dad looked in some distress, but the plastic navigator seemed unmoved by his experience. The roar of the engines seemed like silence after the howling of the gale.

"I've got glue all over my uniform," said the writer.

Conrad said nothing but thought, If I hadn't used too much cement my dad would have bombed Nuremberg in person. Conrad didn't feel strong anymore. He felt weak and shaky.

"Hey. Thanks very much," said his dad. "You saved my life then, you know."

"That's all right," said Conrad. He felt a bit like crying, he didn't know why. He wanted to be home in bed; he wanted to leak back.

He made his way back to the pilot's seat and relieved Towzer at the controls. He read the flickering instruments and turned the great, lumbering bomber on its homeward route.

The sky was dark and empty again after the Christmas trees of Nuremberg. The great plane buzzed slowly through the empty sky; the wind was against them now.

Nuremberg, Nuremberg. They had bombed Nuremberg and now they were coming home. Conrad felt very tired. Nuremberg, he thought. A city bigger than Edinburgh, smaller than Leeds. His grandmother lived in Leeds. He thought of bombers, German bombers bombing Leeds. German bombs crashing through his grandmother's roof. She wouldn't know what was happening. They wouldn't be aiming for his grandmother, but they might hit her all the same. Stop thinking, he said to himself, but he couldn't help it. There had to be grandmothers in Nuremberg too; Conrad wasn't stupid. Had one of his bombs fallen through someone's grandmother's roof? It was a bad thought, and it wouldn't go away. How did bomber pilots stop themselves from thinking bad thoughts on the slow journey home through the quiet empty sky? He reached for Towzer and sank his hand into the comforting warm fur.

"Plane coming up behind!" It was the great writer.

Conrad didn't have time to do anything. A burst of gunfire crashed into the wing of the Lancaster from the unseen Messerschmitt. Then they were alone again, left by the night fighter to struggle and crash. Conrad checked the controls. The oil pressure was falling rapidly on the one good port engine, which was rapidly overheating. If he didn't shut it down, he'd have a fire on his hands. He pulled the feathering toggle and leaned out to watch it splutter to a halt. They were losing height already, at the rate of five hundred feet a minute. They weren't going to get back. They had bought it.

"Get your parachute on, Dad," he said. "We're going to have to jump."

"Oh no," said his dad. "Do we have to?"

"You'll like it," said Conrad. "People pay money to do it. It's a healthy hobby, Dad."

"Oh, cut it out," moaned his dad, struggling to get the straps around his fat body. "Dibs I go first."

"You *are* first," said Conrad. "We've got to jettison the heavy stuff first, and you're the heaviest stuff here."

"But I don't speak German. Can't we wait till we get to France?"

"You'll soon pick it up," said Conrad. To his surprise, he felt quite wide awake and cheerful again. "Open the emergency door."

"Right," said his dad. "Er, what do I do?"

"Well, you sort of jump out of the plane," said Conrad in a sarcastic voice.

"I was afraid it might be something like that," said the great writer. "Then what?"

"You count up to five slowly and pull."

"Well, I can do that all right, I think."

"Get going and do it then," said Conrad.

"Right. Right," said his dad. "See you later then."

"Right," said Conrad.

"Right," said his dad. "Right, I'll just, er . . . I'll just do it now, shall I? Just sort of leap bravely out, eh?"

"YES!!!" howled the exasperated pilot.

"Right, okay then," said the writer. Conrad turned and saw his dad leaning gingerly out.

"I don't really much like the look of it down—waaaagh!" Conrad's dad had made his first parachute jump.

The plane leaped forward as the great weight departed, but it was soon losing height again. Conrad scrabbled under the seat. One parachute. He scrabbled under the navigator's seat for a parachute for Towzer. And found a molded gray plastic model of a parachute.

"Oh, Towzer," he said.

Towzer whined and nuzzled him. Conrad couldn't stand it. He thrust the protesting hairy legs through the straps of his own parachute and tightened them.

"You look like a bundle of old washing, Towzer," he said. Towzer looked seriously alarmed, much as he did when trapped in the kitchen with an imminent bath in store for him.

"It's not a bath, Towzer," said Conrad. "It's more a sort of a walk."

Towzer pricked up his ears and wagged his tail. Before he could do anything else Conrad shoved him through the door, and with a startled yelp Towzer shot out into the night.

Conrad was alone in the plane with nothing but a plastic model parachute. The plane was losing height with every second. He might never see his dad or his Towzer again. He didn't know whether he was over the town or the country, land or water; he didn't know whether there was any chance of surviving a crash landing. He didn't know anything, and it wasn't fair. The war was asking too much of him. He was only a boy.

He peered ahead. Pitch black. Nothing to be seen below. But he must be near the ground now. It would all be over soon. If he died in the crash, did that mean he'd be stuck forever in the war, an unknown casualty, and never leak back into his own world of Parkin and Creamer and the Airfix models? If he died in the crash, maybe he would leak back dead, be found in his bed stone cold with dreadful and mysterious fatal injuries. Well, somebody would be finding out soon.

He checked his instruments. Five hundred feet. He switched on the landing lights. Amazingly, they worked, and he saw the ground heaving and swaying in front of him. He had almost no control of the plane now; its strange lurches had no connection with the way he wrenched the control column to and fro. He saw sky. He saw an upside-down river. He saw a forest standing on its side. He saw cloud, or was it snow? He saw sky again. He saw a road. He saw a snow-covered field, the right way up, rushing toward him at murderous speed. Height twenty feet. Ground speed a hundred miles an hour. He cut the engines and shut his eyes.

The jarring crash roared into his ears. He felt as if he'd been hammered into a dentist's chair with a pile driver. He felt crushed all over, as if the whole world was trying to crash its way into his body. The roaring in his ears grew louder and louder, and suddenly he was floating on a sea of darkness, weightless, beyond space, beyond time. Floating through the dark, endless universe. He didn't know where he was or when he was or who he was. Then the blackness seeped around him like a big black glove and he lost consciousness.

On the Back Step

Conrad was alive. He was cold, and he felt sick, and he hurt all over, but he was alive. Why was he hurting? Why did he feel sick? Was it flu? Surely, surely, if he was alive, he must have leaked back to his own house and his cozy bed? Great writer in the bathroom, mom off to work, Conrad in control? Why was his bed so cold? With an effort he moved his head to look around.

He was lying in thick, snow-covered grass, and the moon was shining on him. He didn't recognize the place. It wasn't his back garden, it wasn't the playground. It certainly didn't look like heaven, at least not the way old

Parkin had described it. Parkin was an old friend of God, and she knew all these things. She reckoned God was in control of everything, but Conrad took all that with a grain of salt. If God was in control, he was making a bit of a mess of things, in Conrad's opinion. He should pack it in and put Conrad in control.

It was surprisingly pleasant to lie in the snow and think about God and the universe. Conrad's brain felt clear and his body felt weak, and it seemed just the right thing to lie there and let his mind wander in the darkness. Without moving his head he could see a clump of trees and a big humpy mound behind them. It was very quiet, very peaceful. No birds, no cars, no chattering little girls talking about dolls and being sick. Just a gentle crackling roar coming from somewhere over to his left, like a garden bonfire.

A garden bonfire, at night, in the snow? That seemed unlikely. Very slowly he turned his aching neck, and saw fifty yards away the huge, gaunt silhouette of the crashed Lancaster, burning quietly away by itself. He was not at home. He hadn't died. He hadn't leaked back. He had survived the crash. He was still in the war.

Suddenly, from over to the left, near the crashed plane, he heard voices. He couldn't make out what they were saying. They weren't English voices. Soon they would be looking for him. He had to move. He tried moving his legs, and it hurt a lot, but he could do it. He was aching all over, but his bones didn't seem to be broken. He got onto his hands and knees. That didn't feel too bad. Then he stood up. He felt dizzy, and the clump of trees lurched toward him sickeningly, but he stood still, and the feeling passed. He had to move. He had to move.

He picked up his left foot and put it down again. Everything was very slow and dreamy; it was like walking under water. Right foot. His head swirled. Left foot. Right foot. The air seemed to be getting thicker. Left foot. Right foot. It was like having your head stuck in a soft, woolly sweater. Left foot. Right foot. Left foot. The trees were really close now. The air was thicker and thicker. Left foot. The darkness came right over him again and he slipped gently forward into the snow on the edge of the trees.

When he woke up again he was in his own back garden. No doubt this time. Trash can. Trellis. Towzer's summer kennel. The big window with the curtains open. The lights were on; he could see his mom and Florence sitting on the sofa. He'd leaked back! It all looked so clear and bright and safe and cozy and warm; the nicest kind of mushiness. His mother was putting yet another patch on the right knee of his pajamas, and Florence was sitting cuddled up to her with two dolls, talking to them. He couldn't hear her voice, but it was a safe bet that the subject was sick.

Conrad moved to within a foot of the window. The television was on. Some soft play about nurses; it might even be one of the great writer's pathetic efforts. A thin, important nurse was sitting at a desk yakking away at a plump, baby-faced, unimportant nurse who was trembling her lips as if her life depended on it. The thin, important nurse slammed a book shut. The face of the dopey, plump nurse filled the screen. A big tear came out of one of her eyes and rolled down her fat baby cheek. Conrad was glad they couldn't see him out there in the dark; they knew that crying enraged him almost as much as kissing, and they'd tease him about it. Another tear rolled down her cheek. Conrad felt cold. Why didn't he knock on the window and

make them let him in? He didn't know, but something was
stopping him. He felt as if he had to stay outside and watch
his family through the window. As he watched, his mother
turned her head toward the glass. Conrad ducked, but
there was no need. He could tell from the look on her face
that she couldn't see out. She was thinking. She couldn't
know he was out there. She must think that he was safe
upstairs in his bed.

But wait a minute. If Conrad was supposed to be
upstairs in his bed, then Fatty Florence should be as well.
And that crying nurses serial was early in the evening.
Where was he supposed to be? His mother turned her head
again, and Conrad saw his dad shamble vaguely into the
room, grind to a halt, and stand staring blankly. Florence
pointed to the screen and said something to the great
writer. Conrad looked at the screen. Aaaargh! Kissing! He
turned his head away and counted up to five.

"Conrad!"

Had they seen him? He looked up sharply. But his mom
was looking toward the hall door expectantly.

Suddenly Conrad felt cold and sick. He didn't want to
see himself come in through that door and sit on the sofa.
Because if that happened, how would he, the Conrad on
the back step, ever get back into his family? Come to that,
if the Conrad in the house came through that door and sat
on the sofa, *who* was he, the Conrad on the back step? He
had to do something, he had to make them see him, he had
to leak back properly.

He took the last step toward the French window, clung
to the handle, watched them turn, and fainted.

The Interrogation

Conrad woke up with a jolt. The light was hurting his eyes and the hard chair he was sitting on hurt his bottom. He blinked.

There were three other people in the room. At a desk in front of him under a bright light sat an extremely pale young man in German officer's uniform, with a hideous scar down his left cheek. He was staring intently at Conrad. Lounging in a chair by his side was another German officer, an older man with a row of medal ribbons, with a tired and wrinkled face. This man did not look like a German, or at least not like the sort of Germans Conrad knew from the comics. As a matter of fact, he looked a bit like the manager of the liquor store supported so loyally by Conrad's dad. (Great writers needed more booze than other men.)

The third man was Conrad's dad. He sat in a hard chair like Conrad's by the wall, and he looked as if he didn't know where he was and didn't much care. Pretty much as usual, in fact, except that his uniform was a disgusting mess. It seemed likely that with his usual skill and foresight in matters physical, Conrad's dad had parachuted into a cesspit. Brown ooze was dripping from his tattered socks and gathering in thick smelly pools on the floor. It was good to have him there, though.

"So," said the pale-faced officer. "You are ready to talk to us now?"

"No," said Conrad, sounding braver than he felt.

"All right," said the pale-faced officer. "We have plenty of time." He smiled at Conrad. It was not a nice smile.

"Where are we?" said Conrad.

The officer giggled and dropped his monocle. "You must know that as well as you know your own name, Flying Officer Pike," he said. "We are in Colditz Castle."

Colditz! Conrad knew all about Colditz. He had seen it a million times on television, he had played the board game at Billy Webb's until he knew the plan like the pattern on his pajamas. And now he was here in person. He knew he was in for a battle of wits, endurance, and imagination that would suit him right down to the ground. He even knew the things to say.

"I'm afraid we shan't be able to stay long, Kapitan," he said with his best sarcastic sneer.

"Arrogant English dog!" snapped Scarface. Conrad

wondered if Towzer had walked in, but before he could ask after his furry friend the officer had recovered his composure. "With regret, we must insist on a prolonged visit. We have . . . so much to learn from each other."

"You'll get nothing out of me," said Conrad, "except my name, rank, and serial number."

"What *is* your number, by the way, little airman?" said the older officer.

"Um . . ." Conrad had forgotten his number. "I can't remember," he said.

"Insubordinate pig-dog!" shrilled Scarface. His left arm was jerking uncontrollably. Conrad knew how he felt. Any minute now he might get on the table and tell Conrad and his dad they had no sympathy or gratitude.

But the officer was made of sterner stuff. "No matter," he said. "We already know it all. Harris's briefing; the protests over the stupid route that was chosen; your little friend Aircraftman Creamer . . . we even know about your *grossmutti* in Leeds."

Conrad was shaken by the scope of their information, but he managed to give a careless, daredevil shrug.

"But what we don't know," said the colonel from the liquor store, "is the name of your fat companion, or the real nature of his mission."

"I'm his dad," said Conrad's dad apologetically. "I didn't want to come at all."

"Silence!" screamed Scarface, starting to twitch again. "Do you dare to jest with the Wehrmacht?"

"But I am his dad," said the great writer. "Sorry. Not my fault."

Scarface's left arm began to jump about again. Conrad and his dad and the colonel from the liquor store watched in silence as he struggled to hold it down with his right hand. Finally he pressed it to the table and weighted it down with a large inkwell in the shape of an eagle.

"You are beginning to exhaust my patience," he whispered through clenched teeth.

"I suppose he might be telling the truth," ventured the older officer. "Perhaps even little British pilots have their papas."

"There is more to it than this," hissed Scarface. "This is something big."

The two interrogators went into a whispering huddle, occasionally looking up and spitting mysterious gobbets of German about the room. Conrad was worried, but his dad looked completely serene. He probably thought he was having one of the boring dreams he so often pressed on the family at breakfast time. As Conrad watched him, he saw an idea gradually take shape, trundle around the rusty wheels, and emerge in the form of speech.

"If this is going to be a bit of a lull," said the great writer, "would it be all right if I went to the toilet?"

"Toilet!" snapped Scarface. "What is this toilet?"

"You know," said the great writer. "Um . . . bathroom. No? Er . . . WC."

"WC? Is this some British code?" The pale interrogator snarled and twitched. He was on to something big, he knew it. The colonel from the liquor store bent and whispered in his ear something that made him go white with fury. "You English pigs! Have you no sense of propriety? Are there no standards in the British Air Force? Have you no self-control? Am I interrogating men or pigs?"

"Pigs don't go to the toilet," said the great writer in a mild tone.

"Shut up! Shut up! Shut up! How can I give the third degree to a prisoner sitting on a lavatory seat?"

The inkwell began to rattle up and down. There was a short pause as they all watched it.

"Well, can I go then?" said Conrad's dad.

The inkwell rattled.

"I always go about this time."

More rattles.

"I'll try not to be too long."

Conrad smiled in spite of the seriousness of the situation. Little did they know. His dad was tackling the situation brilliantly.

"Sorry to go on about it," said the fat writer. "But I think I really must hurry you up. It's a bit urgent."

The inkwell reached a crescendo, and was still. A cunning smile played across the interrogator's cruel features. "Very well," he sneered. "We shall play it your way. First left down the corridor. Guard!!"

Conrad and his interrogators stared at each other in silence as they heard the crash of the door down the corridor. There was a pause, then the muffled voice of the fat writer echoed down the grim stone walls. "Don't think much of your toilet paper. Haven't you got any soft stuff?"

Two hours passed. The interrogation was getting nowhere. Repeated efforts had failed to eject the great writer from his new refuge, his home away from home. And Conrad had survived threats, trick questions, bribes, and curses, without ever remembering his serial number or anything else.

The scar-faced interrogator was nearing the end of his tether.

"Come on, come on, little English dog!" he hissed. "We

know your game. How do you expect us to believe that the British would send over a skinny little runt like you in a sabotaged airplane? It must be espionage! We know all about it already! We just want to hear it from you! Come on! Out with it! What is Operation WC?"

"You won't get anything out of me," said Conrad stubbornly. "As the skeleton said to the toilet."

"That word again!" screamed Scarface. He was staring around wildly and frothing at the mouth.

Suddenly he froze. From the silent echoing corridor came the harsh and mournful sound of a rusty lavatory flush.

Clomp clomp clomp along the corridor.

The German officers turned.

The great writer stood in the doorway with a rueful expression on his face and a broken lavatory chain dangling from his grasp.

"I'm afraid it came off in my hand," he said.

Scarface fell across the table in a dead faint.

"Take them away," said the colonel wearily. "The interrogation is over."

Conrad in Colditz Castle

"What are your plans for escape?" said Conrad.

No answer. The officers lay on their bunks writing letters, carving chess sets, picking their noses, and biting their nails.

"Look," said Conrad. "This is no good. The first duty of a prisoner is to escape. Right or wrong?"

Over in the corner a sordid-looking chap who looked as if he hadn't shaved for a week clapped his hands slowly. Nobody else seemed to take any notice.

"Well," said Conrad. "Why aren't you all escaping?"

"You must be joking," they said. "This is Colditz."

"*I* know it's *Colditz*," said Conrad. "*I'm* not a *fool*, you know. I know all about Colditz."

"Well, why don't you shut up then?" they said.

"Look," said Conrad. "I don't want any of your cheek. I want to escape out of here as soon as possible. I've got to get home, I have."

There was a long silence. The famous prisoners of Colditz went on with their letters and their chess sets and their disgusting habits. Conrad began to get disillusioned.

"Well, I don't know," he said. "I understood that you people were planning daring escapes all the time. Wooden horses! Impersonation stunts!"

They yawned. "Nothing like that?" said Conrad falteringly.

"All sorts of things like that," said the sordid, unshaven one. "The only snag is, they keep catching us, and shooting our heads off, and all sorts of nasty things like that, you see."

"But you're not scared off by a bit of danger, are you?" said Conrad challengingly.

"Well, yes, we are, old man, actually," said the sordid fellow.

"Well all I can say is that I'm mighty disappointed in you," said Conrad. "You're supposed to be an inspiration, a . . . a living legend. That's what you're supposed to be."

"We're fed up with that," they said. "We're just waiting for the war to finish and we'll go home. What's the hurry?"

For a moment, Conrad couldn't think of the answer to that one, and it didn't look as though they'd be very impressed if he could think of one. He climbed up onto a high vacant bunk and lay on it, scowling. Surely the gaunt, self-sacrificing escape officer would be along any minute to question him and sound him out for possible escape bids. Minutes went by. Hours went by. Nothing happened. Conrad had a good long think. Could he spend the rest of the war writing letters, carving chess sets, and picking his nose?

"Dad," he said. "We're not going to spend the rest of the war carving chess sets and picking our noses, are we?"

"Well," said his dad. "We might write a few letters as well."

This was intolerable.

"Look!" said Conrad. "Who's the escape officer here? Don't tell me there isn't one because I know there is, I've seen it all on the box."

There was a long silence. Then the sordid, unshaven one rolled over on his bunk and scowled at Conrad with bloodshot eyes. "As a matter of fact," he said, "I'm the escape officer."

"I don't believe it," said Conrad. "He's not really, is he?"

"He is," they said.

"Right," said Conrad. "Back to square one. What . . . are . . . your . . . plansforescapeeh???"

"Look, old man," said the escape officer. "We've tried everything. We haven't got any more plans for escape, we're fed up with the whole issue."

"Pathetic!" said Conrad.

A fat and walruslike colonel from the Marines blinked dopily as he looked up from his model of Notre Dame in human moustache clippings. "You could tell him about the glider."

All the officers laughed. "Yeah, tell him about the glider, Gavin."

"Oh, come *on*," said the sordid escape officer.

"Tell me about the glider," said Conrad. This sounded more like it. "Come on, tell me about it. I insist."

"Well," said the escape officer wearily. "The idea is, we all save up a lot of bits of wood and stuff and build a glider in the attic, and then when it's ready two of us get in it and glide off the roof and over the outside fence."

"That's a great idea," said Conrad. "Whose show is it?"

"Nobody's," said the escape officer. "The chap who thought it up was raving mad, he's been carted away."

"I'll take it over," said Conrad. "I'll show you bunch of loafers. Who's going to join me?"

Silence.

"I said: who's going to join me?" repeated the intrepid aviator. His voice sounded high and weedy, even to himself.

"Look here, old chum," said the walrus colonel. "We're terribly impressed with your enthusiasm, but it's just not on."

Conrad was in a rage. "You have no bravery or imagination!" he screeched, jumping up and down on his bunk. The walrus colonel, dislodged by the vibrations, fell out of his bunk onto the floor and rolled about in a bewildered manner.

"I, Conrad," shouted Conrad, "am going to build this glider single-handed!"

They all stared at him in stupefaction.

"And my dad," he added, "is going to help me!"

Colditz was just like school: nasty, cold, boring, and full of people who told you what to do all the time. It even looked like school with its tall windows and its big yard, whose features became familiar in every detail: the coal heap, the cycle sheds, the huge, steel barred gate through which the delivery trucks came every day, the stone steps leading up to the heavy wooden door beyond which lay the German officers' quarters, the door through which no prisoner could pass. Just like the door leading to the faculty room in school. Beyond that door, the German officers would be lolling about in comfy chairs smoking pipes and reading papers, just like teachers; their toilets would have velvet seats and golden chains like the faculty toilets in Conrad's school (so he had imagined them), with the Commandant's private toilet the most luxurious of all, a sort of paradise convenience like the one Headmaster Harris was supposed to have, so splendid it could hardly be imagined by ordinary prisoners or boys. Perhaps it would have an aquarium full of tropical fish, and an electrically operated seat which played lovely music in stereo every time you pressed the button.

There was lots of time for thinking thoughts like this in Colditz, Conrad found. Lots of time waiting for something to happen, wandering around the exercise yard thinking great thoughts while his fellow prisoners played soccer. That was like school too. Conrad didn't know what was the matter with them. Instead of planning heroic escapes, they would charge about the yard playing soccer with scrunched-up bags, pieces of coal, anything. They were a great disappointment. It was no use asking them to play army; they had clearly had enough of it. Conrad was making the gradual discovery that it wasn't just his mom and dad who weren't keen on violence and killing and army and war. Here was a whole prison yard full of people who were supposed to be British heroes, and they were no use at all. Sometimes he would go up to one of them and try to get him going.

"Look," Conrad would say. "When the doors open to let the trucks through, there are only two armed guards on the gate. Why don't we rush them and overpower them, and swipe their uniforms, and drive off in the trucks?"

A great plan. Simple. Violent. Exciting. Inspiring. But what would the great British prisoners say to it?

"Buzz off, Conrad, I'm supposed to be keeping goal."

Or: "Do you think it would help if I took his bishop?"

Or: "Can you think of anything exciting I could put in this letter to my aunt?"

"Yes!" Conrad would shriek. "Tell her you're going to overpower the guards, steal their uniforms, and drive off in their truck!"

"Be a good sport, beat it, Conrad," they'd say.

"Stop fooling around, and let me get on with my nose-picking."

What a bunch! Conrad was disgusted with them.

But the glider was gradually taking shape. Every day, after roll call in the yard, Conrad would take his ragged old towel to the washroom, turn left instead of right, climb a rusty old water pipe, squat on top of the water tank, and pull himself up through a narrow gap into the attic. He would shut his eyes, take a deep breath, and open them. And there would be his glider.

It was enormous. Even in its unfinished state, it filled the attic completely, and it wouldn't be possible to fit the wings till they got it up on the roof. To get it on the roof they'd have to smash through the ceiling, which would be both noisy and impossible, but Conrad wasn't worried about that. By now he was used to noisy and impossible things. Conrad was invincible. He had had a lot of trouble getting any help with his glider. You'd have thought that all the fellows would rally around to this heroic task, but most of them had just laughed and gone back to their soccer and their horrible habits. But the sordid escape officer had reluctantly scrambled up every day to help him (because it was his job), and Conrad's dad had allowed himself to be lugged puffing and grumbling up the rusty pipe (because he was Conrad's dad).

There, under Conrad's shrill commands, uttered as he danced about the attic, leaped on and off piles of old boxes, snapped his fingers, and kicked old bits of wood around in showers of dust, the thin escape officer and the fat writer had helped the great glider builder to construct his craft. It was made of even stranger and more ramshackle materials than even Conrad had used before: wood, metal, cardboard, old sheets, bedsprings, towels, newspapers, window frames, shoelaces, glass, string, and oilskin.

And now it was nearly complete. The day before, under cover of a Prison Sports Day and Three-Day Equestrian Event (a complicated entertainment featuring officers as pantomime horses), Conrad and the escape officer had managed to sneak two bikes out of the cycle shed and get them up to the attic in bits. Then, while the great writer had scratched his bald brains in bewilderment and admiration, the escape officer and the boy genius had reassembled the bikes to provide the motive power to get the glider going. A two-man pedal plane!

Looking at it now, Conrad couldn't quite imagine it flying. This cranky contraption was somehow going to get itself onto the roof, the wings were going to fit themselves on so that they would hold fast for the length of the glide, and then Conrad and his dad, by pedal power alone, would have to get up enough speed to rocket the monstrous invention off the roof and into a fifty-yard glide, losing height all the way, but still keeping it far enough off the ground to clear the sixteen-foot outer wall. That was all. After that it would be easy. The only trouble was, he just couldn't quite see it in his mind's eye.

Never mind. Who knows what would happen? He had survived a crash landing on the Nuremberg raid; he could survive this. He could survive anything—and maybe he wouldn't even have to. Any time now he might leak back for good into his own cozy home, and deep down inside he knew he'd be glad to. He was tired of German prison food, greasy soup and cold cabbage. Too much like school dinners at their worst. He was tired of the cold nights in his hard bunk. And in his secret mind he was tired of being a man among men; he would like to be a little boy again. He was missing Towzer; he yearned for that warm fur against him. He hoped Towzer was all right, and tears lurked at the back of his eyes as he thought of his Towzer dog, puzzled and lonely, trotting around aimlessly in occupied territory, with no one to open his dogfood and make his bed up and play stick with him.

There was a creak and a scrabble in the corner and a mouse ran for safety. The sordid escape officer's gloomy face appeared in the gap between the floorboards. Conrad gave him a hand up.

"You're late," said Conrad sternly.

"I was just finishing a letter," said the escape officer.

"You're always wasting your time like that," said Conrad. "Writing love letters to your girl friends. Call yourself an escape officer? More like a Big Drip, I'd say."

"Everyone's entitled to their opinion," said the escape officer.

"I mean," said Conrad, striding around and accidentally kicking a hole in the glider's fuselage, "if you were a proper escape officer, you'd get up here on time and work a bit harder, and then you could get back home and see all your rotten girl friends, if that's what you really want to do. Sounds mad to me, but it must be better than writing letters to them all the time."

"Oh, cut it out," said the escape officer. "You're kicking your glider to bits. Anyway, I'm not sure I want to get home all that much; I've soured on my girl friends a bit. All they write about is their bacon ration."

"I can see the point of that," said Conrad. "Well, if you went home, you'd be back with your own unit again. Fly on some more glorious raids. How about that, eh?"

"Oh, thank you very much indeed," said the escape officer. "I think I'd just as soon stay here and let the other guys win the war."

Conrad was speechless. What an escape officer. *He* would not show up in a good light when Conrad wrote his great history of the war.

Clattering and moaning from down below announced the ascent of the fat writer. Conrad and the escape officer heaved and tugged his stout body through the gap.

"Take it easy," said the writer. "This is the only body I've got."

"Wouldn't have it as a gift," said Conrad. "Get working."

They jacked the wheels up and levered Conrad's dad into the back seat. Then Conrad leaped lightly into the pilot's seat, pulling down his goggles to get into the mood.

"Right," said Conrad. "Pedal!" The fat hairy legs and the skinny knobbly legs pushed on the pedals, faster and faster, the fiendishly ingenious gears (designed and patented by the great Conrad) clicked and connected, and the wheels whirred around so fast that a cloud of dust filled the attic, and two mice who had come out of their holes to watch were flung flat on their backs against the wall.

"It works!" shouted Conrad. "And tonight, it'll fly!" He leaped out of the cockpit and danced around the attic.

"You," he said to the escape officer, "are in charge of getting the Nazi officer uniforms, and *you*," he said to his dad, "are in charge of getting the food supplies and false passports. My responsibility will be blowing a hole in the roof to get the glider up there, I don't know exactly how I'll do it, but I'll think of something, don't worry. Colonel Walrus will organize the riot to draw the attention of the guards, and at 0015 hours exactly the great . . . what are you looking at?"

They were looking at him with a strange expression. What was it? Long-suffering irritation? Sympathy? A sort of I-know-better-than-you look? Something of all of these, and Conrad didn't like it. It made him feel weak and small; it made him feel less of a genius and more of a little boy.

"It's not on, Conrad," said the escape officer.

"Not on?" shouted Conrad. "What are you talking about?" But his shout sounded weak and reedy.

"You know it won't really fly," said the escape officer. "If we ever got it up on the roof, you'd just about manage to pedal it to the edge, then it'd topple over and fall all the way down to the yard. Splat."

"Want a bet?" said Conrad aggressively.

"You haven't got anything I want," said the escape officer.

Conrad looked at the glider and suddenly seemed to see it through the eyes of the grownups. What a flimsy, ramshackle contraption it was. His courage weakened, but he had to keep his end up.

"Well, look," he said. "If it was such a hopeless idea, why did you both come up here with me every day and help me build it, eh? What about that, then?"

They looked at him sadly.

"We just wanted you to have a hobby," said Conrad's dad. "We didn't want you to pine away. Sorry."

Conrad looked at the escape officer and saw the same horrible, sorry-for-little-Conrad expression on his face too.

"It was good fun building it, though, Conrad," he said.

For a moment Conrad thought he was going to cry, but just in time he felt the familiar, warm, homey feeling of rage and disgust flooding through his veins.

"You!" he screeched, "are a rotten, useless pair of goof-offs! And I, Conrad, am going to *show you!*"

Sleep-leaking

In the middle of the night Conrad got up. He slithered down the wooden post without disturbing the walrus colonel, who was rolling from side to side puffing and blowing and muttering to himself about getting his golf handicap down. The air was thick with the sleeping breath of the big men. Dark, heaving silhouettes, little creaking sounds, sighs, and snores. Conrad felt strange. He wasn't quite sure whether he was asleep or awake, and he didn't know where he was going. He felt his way toward a door and went through it.

It seemed that he was on his own landing at home, warm carpet under his bare feet. Had part of his house come to Colditz? He tried to think, but he couldn't get his brain to work properly. There was something he had to do, but he wasn't sure what. Had he gotten up to go to the bathroom? He couldn't seem to remember where it was. He found himself walking along the dark landing, hearing the familiar snore like a sound from long ago, when he was a little boy. Was he still a little boy? If only his mind would work. He didn't know what he was or where he was or who he was.

He went into a little room. It was warm in the room. There was a bed in the corner and someone was in it. He bent over the bed and heard soft breathing, smelled soft, sweet breath. It was something that he ought to recognize, but he couldn't. It was nice, though. He pulled the covers back and got in, and started telling Florence how he was planning to blow the roof off the attic and get the glider up. It was important to explain it to her properly, but she didn't seem to be able to understand his exposition, even though he went over and over it. He wasn't sure whether the words were coming out right; it seemed to be an effort to move his jaws and produce the right sounds, but he had to go on and do it. His little sister turned from side to side, and started to moan in her high, piping voice. He tried to say, "Please shut up, Florence, it's hard enough as it is," but the words came out in a jumble. He was getting into a tangle with the bedclothes, and he felt hot and trapped.

Someone was in the room, two big figures. "What's the matter, Conrad?" they said. "What are you doing in here?"

He tried to explain but he didn't seem to be able to talk the language.

"Did you want to go to the john?"

He couldn't tell them. It was so much effort. They were

helping him out of Florence's bed and taking him along the landing. It was all so stupid, he wanted to laugh. They stood him in the john. He tried to talk, he tried to make them understand it wasn't what he wanted, but it was all too much effort. It was nice, though, being led around, not having to think or make people do things. He let them lead him back to his room, and he flopped impatiently down into his cozy bed.

"Are you all right, now, Conrad?" they said, but it was too much trouble to tell them, and anyway, he could feel himself going; there was no stopping it. He was leaking back into the war.

In the big bedroom Joe Pike was already drifting into sleep.

"Put the light out," he mumbled.

"Aren't you worried?" said his wife. "I mean, sleepwalking. There must be something disturbing him. Don't you think?"

Pause.

"Are you awake?"

"Of course I'm awake," said the writer, drifting back into semiconsciousness.

"Do you think I should take him to the doctor?"

"No."

"Really? Aren't you worried?"

"No. Sleepwalking? Everyone does that."

"I never did."

"Used to do it all the time when I was a kid," mumbled Joe Pike. "It's fun, actually."

Conrad's mother sat staring at the wall for a few minutes, then put the light out.

The Night
of the Glider

Conrad was awake. His brain felt clear and hard again.
The stone floor was hard and cold under his feet, the chill
running up his legs, but he didn't care. He knew where he
was and what he had to do now, and he knew he could do
it, his body tuned up and springy like a steel machine. The
corridor was dark, but he knew which way to go; his feet
knew everything without any messages from his brain. At
the end of the corridor he found himself right up against
the huge, heavy, solid door. Massive bars. Double locks.
German strength against British cunning.

What did you do with locks? Conrad knew. He reached

into his sock, not knowing why he was doing it, and pulled out a strip of metal. It was the nameplate from Towzer's old collar. On one side it said TOWZER PIKE with fancy scrolls all around it. On the other side it gave Conrad's address and phone number. Conrad turned it Towzer side up and thrust it into the top lock. All he had to do was press. He could feel the spring bunch into itself, then the lock sprang back with a sweet click. He turned the nameplate over and wiggled it into the bottom lock. This one was tighter. Conrad put both thumbs on the fancy scrolls and pushed sideways, and the second lock shuddered back. Conrad silently swung the great door open, and stepped into the yard.

The yard was silent, empty, moonlit, and the air was freezing. Just before Conrad had time to wonder what he was doing there, the thought was there in his mind, clear and bright as a new penny. The trucks. He had to get something from the trucks. But first he had to stand still. Why? He didn't know, but he knew he had to obey his instincts all the time now. He stood in the doorway shivering for ten seconds, then he heard the regular, clumping steps of the guard. Conrad drew back into the darkness and watched the dark silhouette clump past like a clockwork toy, jerking its head from right to left every four steps, never pausing, never varying.

Conrad waited till the clumping of the clockwork boots had almost died away, then darted silently across the yard to the trucks. There were six of them. It was in the trucks, whatever it was, and as soon as he drew near to the huge, gaunt shapes he knew that the signals were coming from the fourth one.

It had been raining and the knots in the tar-coated rope that held down the tarpaulin had shrunk tight. Definitely the sort of knot which in normal circumstances he would howl for the fat writer to untie. But now Conrad felt his hands and wrists all strong and steely, his fingers blunt and hard as Grandad's tools. He attacked the knots purposefully, knowing instinctively which strand would yield the secret, and in seconds the ropes were lying limp and useless.

He scrambled up over the tailgate. Inside the truck it was pitch dark as soon as the tarpaulin flapped back behind him. That didn't matter. His hands and feet were leading him again. Creep three steps, then reach out upward to the left. There it was. A bulky parcel that he knew he had to touch very gently. Plastic explosive. So that was what he had come for. Tucking it gently down under his pajamas and cradling it against his chest with his left hand, Conrad used his right to swing himself lightly down over the tailgate.

Then he found himself crouching under the truck. What had made him do that? There was nobody around.

He waited, and then heard: clump clump clump clump. CLUMP CLUMP CLUMP CLUMP.

Of course. It was the clockwork guard again with his jerky head: clump clump clump clump, RIGHT LEFT, clump clump clump clump . . . and so on.

There was a big lump of coal under the truck, and Conrad felt tempted to whang it over and score a direct hit on the clockwork guard's helmet. Once, throwing an apple core away in the playground, he had turned with horror to see old Parkin coming out on playground duty with her cup of tea, watched powerless as the apple core arched through its inevitable trajectory, like a doomed missile, landing splosh right in Parkin's tea and splattering it everywhere. Parkin had refused to believe he hadn't done it on purpose. As if he was that good a shot! When he threw balls at coconuts he was as likely to hit the spectators as the target. But he knew now that if he picked up that lump of coal, it would home in on the clockwork guard's head like a guided missile.

He willed himself to keep still. CLUMP CLUMP CLUMP CLUMP, clump clump clump clump clump clump clump clump . . .

Conrad strained his ears.

Silence.

He flitted across the yard like a skinny, pajamaed ghost, swung the great door open, shut it behind him, and Towzered the locks fast again. Now for the attic.

He found it surprisingly easy to clamber up the rusty pipe still with one hand cradling the bundle of explosive. The glider was there, waiting. It looked great. It looked somehow much more of a possibility than it had done before: the newspapers had stiffened and stretched and strengthened as if they knew they were going to have to ride the breeze; the cellophane on the cockpit appeared to have hardened; the wheels looked like real glider wheels. It was like the night of the tank. Under the fantastic power of Conrad's iron will, the physical world was changing into what he wanted it to be. Conrad would prevail!

Now for some brainwork. Where to lay the charges? On the roof, that's what they'd said. But wait a minute. If he blew the roof off, what would the glider stand on for its takeoff? Thin air? They were all idiots—either that, or they hadn't thought the thing through properly. What now?

It was a real problem, but Conrad wasn't daunted by it. He picked up a screwdriver and shoved it through a crack in the wall, then pressed his face up close. Through the slit he could see the roof line sloping gently downward, then flattening. And it was facing outward and it was still only fifty yards from the outer fence. *That* was it! Blow the *wall* out, not the *roof!* Of *course!*

He had seen *The Guns of Navarone* twice on TV, so setting the charges was no problem for the master escapist. In less than five minutes he had set six explosive charges at strategic points on the wall, and led an electrical wire back from the wall to the glider's cockpit. Then he rested for a moment, leaning against the sturdy fuselage he had designed. Electrical work was good, very interesting, almost as good as army, and he hadn't realized he knew so much about it. Conrad the great electrician. Definitely an idea. He would think about that some more when he got out of this war.

All set then?

No.

The uniforms!

It was no use expecting that droopy dead loss of an escape officer to carry out his part of the plan. He was snoring in his bed, dreaming, no doubt, of his three terrible girl friends. I hope he wakes up screaming, thought Conrad. Serve him right, he has no sympathy or consideration, I have to do all the work in this prison, everybody else treats it like a hotel, I don't know what prisoners of war are coming to these days.

Even as he jigged up and down muttering, he knew what he was going to do. Often as he had clambered up the pipe he had noticed a passage going off sideways, dark and rat-infested, but a good foot high: the gap between ceilings of the first floor and the floorboards of the second. A dauntless skinny genius could cover the whole building by following the trail of electrical cables, mice, and dead birds that lay in this no-man's-land between downstairs and upstairs.

He buttoned his pajamas up tight, clambered halfway down the rusty pipe, pushed away a screen of lath and plaster, took a deep breath, and slithered sideways into the dark hole. It had a strong smell, musty and sweetish and throat-tickling, but a boy who had endured years of junior schools had smelled much worse smells than that. He started to crawl, the mice fleeing before him as he picked his way. There were openings in several directions, but Conrad seemed to know the one he had to take. He followed the main cable.

Apart from the mice and dead bats, and the labyrinthine complexity of it, it was not unlike the attic at home. Huge wooden joists running parallel into black infinity; thin, nearly translucent lath and plaster between them. So thin it wouldn't even stand the weight of the skinniest prisoner in Colditz. Conrad had to keep to the joists, following the great snaky twists of power cable that reminded Conrad of the middle section of his plastic kit on *How your body works*.

As he wormed his way farther and farther along, he could feel the warmth coming up through the lath and plaster. He must be over the centrally heated part now, where the German officers lived, pigging it in luxury while the British heroes shivered in their socks. Not far to go now.

Ow! He had hit his nose. Right in his path was a big sack full of hard lumpy stuff. Coal, it must be. Who would leave a sack of coal up here? Somebody's secret supply, it must be, or someone's black market stock in trade, to be sold later when the fuel ran out and the weather got even colder. Conrad had a feeling that this sack would come in handy, and dragged it another few yards behind him. Then he stopped. He stopped because he had to, because this had to be the place. He couldn't see much, but little bright squiggles of light in the lath and plaster told him that he must be above a lighted room. He applied his eye to one of the biggest of the cracks and peered down.

He couldn't make out what it was, at first. A round, shiny black ball divided neatly into two by a white line, with two pink handles, too small for easy handling, on either side? Then a hand came up and adjusted a monocle, and suddenly Conrad knew. He was looking directly down on the shiny brilliantined head of Scarface, the Nazi interrogator! Conrad stared down, fascinated. What was Scarface doing, awake on his own in the lonely hours of the night? Planning new torture techniques? Plotting to discredit his superiors? Conrad would put nothing past him.

Scarface was writing something—or perhaps he was drawing something. If Conrad looked very closely he could see what it was. He strained his eye at the crack of light, and puzzled for a long time, and then he saw.

Scarface was doing a dot-to-dot puzzle.

Not a map, not a secret plan, not an execution order. He was joining the dots. It didn't even look like a very hard one; it looked like the sort that Conrad had grown out of and Florence liked, the sort that Conrad would only do when he was very fed up, or ill, or needing something very, very simple to rest his brain.

Maybe that's what Scarface needed. Maybe, thought Conrad with an odd, unwelcome lurch of sympathy, maybe he gets very tired of being a hard and ruthless interrogator. Maybe it's a strain keeping it up. Poor old Scarface and his dot-to-dots.

Enough of this. This wasn't going to get any gliders

flying. The strength began to surge up Conrad's wiry arms. He clasped the sack of coal firmly against his body and crashed off the joist straight through the lath and plaster, scoring a direct hit with the coal sack on Scarface's head. The interrogator collapsed without a sound, with Conrad on top of him quite unhurt. So much for Scarface!

Conrad lay still for a moment, but no one came. Perhaps they were used to strange sounds from the interrogator's office: a man who played dot-to-dot in the middle of the night might have many eccentricities. Conrad got up and lugged his victim across the floor, then stripped him of his uniform. The interrogator looked even more pathetic and vulnerable in his Wehrmacht Issue winter underwear. Mind you, thought Conrad, looking in the vain interrogator's mirror, I don't look too brilliant in his outerwear.

He appraised himself briefly. Why were his shoulders so narrow? The uniform hung off at either side, and the eagles on the epaulettes looked like a couple of dead parrots. Luckily the interrogator had a waist almost as skinny as Conrad's, but there was something not quite right about the trousers even when Conrad had rolled the bottoms up three times. The cap, however, was very impressive. Smart and ruthless. It came down over his eyes, and Conrad couldn't see a thing from under it unless he tilted his head back so far he nearly broke his neck—but let it pass, he said to himself. These problems often sort themselves out; it might shrink or he might grow to fill it, and in any case it was better than a school uniform.

Now. Scarface must have another uniform, a showoff like that would be bound to. Conrad ransacked his wardrobe, and found an outfit for his dad that looked even smarter than his own. He packed it in Scarface's dainty leather attache case, then opened Scarface's door, leaving the informally clad victim still fast asleep on his office floor.

A bare corridor. At the end, another door. Nobody challenged Conrad, and the door at the far end opened instantly and soundlessly. He was in the yard. Silent. Deserted. No alarm, no clockwork guards. He walked boldly across the cobbles, feeling in his uniform pocket. His fingers closed on a key, as he knew they must. No need to Towzer the door this time; the locks slipped back like oiled silk.

In the prisoners' quarters the British officers snored on, lost in their dreams of God's country and home cooking. Little did they know what great deeds were under way. Conrad stood by his dad's bunk. His dad was sleeping like a baby on his side, with both hands under his cheek and his knees pulled up to his chin, blowing bubbles. It was a shame to disturb him, but Conrad was ruthless.

"Wake up, Dad," he said. "Your hour has come."

"What?" said his dad. "Is it breakfast? I'll be down in a minute," and he turned onto his back and went straight to sleep again, letting out a huge, rumbling snore.

"Dad!!" hissed Conrad. "Wake up! Escape time!"

"Not escaping today," muttered the great writer. "Escape later. Got to gather me strength for a bit, lots to do today. Change me library books, for one thing."

Was ever a great escape begun in such an undignified way? *Library* books! The dozy man must think he's at home, Conrad realized.

"DAD! We're in *Colditz!* Get up! The glider flies at dawn!"

The great writer suddenly sat up straight and banged his head on the bunk above. "What what what what," he said.

Before he could fall down again, Conrad seized him by

the pajama collar. "Get up and get your disguise on. We're all ready for takeoff."

The writer blinked at his son. "What are you wearing those funny clothes for?" he said. "Take it back to the store, it's too big for you."

Conrad would have been insulted if he hadn't known how slowly that rusty brain worked in the mornings. "Wait till we see yours," he said.

Five exhausting minutes later, Conrad's dad was standing unsteadily by his bunk, dressed in Scarface's best Sunday uniform. He looked even sillier than Conrad. He could only fasten half the trouser buttons and none of the tunic buttons. Great, soft, rounded lumps of writer were sticking out everywhere from the smart gray serge. Scarface's hat sat like a shiny wart on the top of his head. Conrad's dad held it steady with one finger on the top, which gave him a disgustingly coy and dancing-school appearance, contrasting wildly with the rolls of flab on every side.

"How do I look?" said the writer.

Conrad gritted his teeth. "You'll do," he said.

They were ready.

Conrad looked around the den of sleeping men. Goodbye, sordid escape officer. Goodbye, Colonel Walrus. Goodbye, chess players, letter writers, and nose pickers. He had despised them all to a man, but now that he was leaving them they seemed all right. This war seemed to be all leaving places and leaving people. Still, he had to show them.

"Come on, Dad," he said.

Up the stairs to the washroom, up the rusty water pipe, squat on the water tank, up through the narrow gap, get the pulley, heave up his dad. He seemed to have done it a million times; he'd never forget how to do it, all his life.

He stuffed his protesting father into his seat in the gleaming glider, then took his own seat with leisurely, icy calm. Just by his right hand was the switch that would fire the explosive charge in the wall. His feet were braced on the pedals and he hoped his dad's were as well. Conrad had plunked them into place, but when the moment came he had no confidence that his dad would not drift off into one of his trances.

When the moment came . . . Why wasn't it the moment now? He wasn't frightened, was he? What was he waiting for? His hand trembled over the switch . . .

Then behind, and below him, he heard an extraordinary sound: saucepans, clattering boots, hoarse shouts, and then the ear-rotting sound of Englishmen's voices uplifted in song:

> *Knees up, Mother Brown,*
> *Knees up, Mother Brown,*
> *Under the table you must go,*
> *Ee eye, ee eye, ee eye oh!*
> *If I catch you bending,*
> *I'll saw your legs right off . . .*

Conrad waited until the unearthly caterwauling was augmented by the clatter of German boots and rifles and harsh Teutonic curses echoing up from the yard, then with one smooth movement he pulled the goggles down over his eyes and pressed the switch.

PFLUMMMMPH!

Conrad watched open-mouthed as the entire wall blew outward in slow motion with a sound like an enormous boot being lifted out of an enormous bog. For a moment he could see nothing, then the dust swirling madly around him cleared for long enough for him to be able to see the sky, the sloping roof, and the outer fence beyond.

"Pedal, Dad!" he screamed, and the great model glider surged forward and accelerated down the gently sloping roof. Conrad could hear a strange wailing sound, realized it came from the great writer, who must have woken up now sufficiently to be terrified, then the glider dipped alarmingly. They were off the roof, nothing but air to keep them up now, and hurtling straight for the top of the fence. Conrad pulled desperately on the toggles and shut his eyes.

"Aaaargh!"

It was his dad again.

"My bottom's hanging out through the floor!"

Conrad opened his eyes. They were alive! The fence had disappeared! They must have gotten over it, leaving most of the undercarriage and perhaps the seat of the great writer's trousers on the wire. Now they were skimming silently along (apart from the moans from the back seat) about thirty feet up, with Colditz behind them and who knew what ahead.

It looked like long grass below; this time they would get a soft landing, wheels or no wheels. Then they would have to get out of the glider and put as much distance between them and Colditz as they could. It would surely only be minutes until the guards quelled the riot in the yard and realized their real task. Conrad eased the toggles and took the glider on a gentle landing course.

"Watch your bum, Dad!"

"I *beg* your pardon, Conrad! . . . Ooh! . . . Ouch! . . . Hey! You're doing it on—Ouch! . . . Aarrrrgh!"

Conrad and his dad had landed.

German Boots

Conrad wasn't sure how long they had been going, but it was bright daylight now. Both he and his dad were sweating in the sunlight. They had stopped for one short rest to finish the last of their emergency chocolate, sitting in a patch of buttercups under a big tree; it had seemed strangely like a picnic. It didn't seem right for the Germans to have buttercups—innocent, friendly flowers. The Krauts probably called them by some snarly, guttural name, but they looked just as shiny and yellow for all that. If Florence had been there, she would have been holding them under everybody's chin, and if Towzer had been there he would have flopped out all over them, marking his territory to defend as he always did on picnics, barking for his piece of chocolate.

Towzer. Conrad had been half-consciously looking out for his furry body and periscope tail ever since they had been walking; he had this feeling that Towzer had been trotting about sniffing and whining around the camp perimeter ever since they had been imprisoned, waiting for them to escape and make everything all right for him. But there was no sign of him. Perhaps he had been captured too. Perhaps . . . perhaps his parachute hadn't opened. Conrad didn't want to think about that. Of course Towzer must be all right.

On they went. Left, right, left right, left right, left right. He was hot but he wasn't tired, his jackboots thudding rhythmically on the hard earth, his dad shambling along patiently by his side. There was a farmhouse they had to find; it was a long way away, but they were going in the right direction. That was all he knew and that was all he needed to know.

Left right, left right, left right.
Left . . . left. I had a good job but I left.
Left right, left right, who's gonna take you out tonight?
Left . . . left . . . had a good job but I left.

Oh be *kind* to your *poor* feathered *friends*, POM POM,
For a *duck* may be *some*body's brooooooo-ther,
He *lives* all *alone* in a *swamp*, POM POM,
Where the weather's *cold* and *damp*, POM-POM-POM,
Oh you *may* think that *this* is the *end*, POM POM,
Well it *is*.

They hadn't seen a soul all morning. No German guards. No policemen. No peasants. No dogs. Just an occasional rabbit. They had managed the first stage with amazing skill and luck. Now all they needed, it seemed, was endurance.

Left . . . left . . . had a good job but I left.

Oh the *high*er up the *moun*tain, the *green*er grows the *grass*,
Here comes an *el*ephant, *sli*ding on his . . .
*High*er up the *moun*tain, the *green*er grows the *grass*,
Here comes an *el*ephant, *sli*ding on his . . .
*High*er up the *moun*tain, the *green*er grows the *grass*,
Here comes an elephant, sliding on his . . .
Links . . . links . . . links recht links!
LINKS RECHT LINKS RECHT LINKS RECHT LINKS!

What was all that now? Must be German for "left right." How had it come into his head? Automatic message transmitted through his jackboots? Conrad didn't know. It made him feel strange. These jackboots were just the thing for marching in, hot as they were. They gleamed in the sunlight and made his calves feel powerful and strong. The iron-tipped heels smacked down satisfyingly into the beaten earth.

Links . . . links . . . links recht links . . .

His uniform seemed to have adapted itself to his body as well, as the morning had warmed up and worn on. It felt snug and smart, holding his waist tight, his back straight as a column of steel. He threw his shoulders back and swung his arms as he marched, full of joy, the sun on his face, the birds singing, the great trees spreading their wings over him. He felt fine.

He glanced sideways at the great writer. *His* uniform hadn't adapted itself to *his* squat body. Conrad's dad looked, if possible, worse than before. He had burst two more buttons on his trousers, his shirt was hanging out, and Conrad could see occasional glimpses of the fat writer's dreaded hairy belly button. Disgusting. Outrageous. The man was an insult to his uniform. Worse than that. What was worse than that? The words came unbidden into Conrad's head: A disgrace to the beloved Fatherland.

The *father*land? What was that now? It couldn't be . . . *Germany,* could it?

Conrad shook his head, snapped his fingers, and danced about a bit.

"What's that?" said his dad. "Hitler imitation? You've got to froth at the mouth and bite the carpet too, you know."

Conrad laughed. His dad was all right. He was all right. Conrad was himself again.

"This sun is hot, you know," he told his dad.

"Is it?" said his dad, mopping his brow. "You could have fooled me."

"What I mean," said Conrad, hopping impatiently, "is you've got to watch it. It can do funny things to your brain."

"Right," said his dad. "I'll be on the lookout for that."

They walked on for a while, each feeling pleased to be with the other and not alone.

Left . . . left . . . left right left . . .

Conrad stopped. "What's that?" he said.

"What's what?" said the great writer, staring into the middle distance with the eager alertness of a stunned ox.

"*Listen*," said Conrad. They listened.

Far off but getting louder was a mechanical sound, even in the distance too big and powerful for a truck or an armored car. It was coming their way.

"We've got to split up," said Conrad.

"Oh dear, have we? I'd much rather not," said his dad. "You seem to be rather more effective than me in these crisis situations."

"I've got a funny feeling about this one," said Conrad, and indeed "funny feeling" was hardly enough to describe the buzzing in his brain and the pounding in his chest. "You'll be all right, Dad. It's me I'm not so sure about."

"Well, where am I supposed to go? Sorry to be so useless, but I can't seem to follow me nose like you can."

Conrad found himself rooting about in his inside pocket. He pulled out a crumpled piece of paper. A map. A map of where they were going. With Colditz at the bottom and a farmhouse near the top.

"There you are, Dad," he said. "You take this. Go off to the right through the trees. I've got to go straight on."

His dad took the map without a murmur.

"Go on, then, get going," said Conrad in a high squeaky voice, half hoping that his dad would refuse to go, stand shoulder to shoulder with him to face what was coming.

"Sure you'll be all right?" said his dad.

"Get going, quick!" squeaked Conrad. Before he could dodge, his father gave him a quick kiss on the cheek, and with a pang of fear and regret Conrad watched the fat writer shamble off into the trees.

Now what? What did he have to do? Run off to the left to confuse the searchers? Double back the way he had come? There seemed no point in either course; the threatening rumble ahead of him was louder by the second. And there was more than that. Conrad *knew* that he had to stay. The feeling was so strong and solid in his brain that there was no question of doing anything else. This was the right thing. Whatever happened, he had to stay standing right in the middle of the path.

As he stood there, he realized that something was happening to him. The fear was going, draining down out of his stomach and down through his boots. He was beginning to get the strong feeling again. His jackboots felt good. Tight and close and shiny. He stamped them on the ground.

Recht. Links. Good boots. He placed them firmly astride, put his hands behind his back, and felt his chest swell out his tunic, which fitted him so well it was like a mold that Conrad had been poured into.

Sun on his face.

Birds in the trees.

Rumbling louder and louder.

Conrad stood firm. He didn't care. He could do anything. Then around the corner a gigantic German Tiger tank came thundering toward him, the turret open, German helmets glinting in the sun.

Konrad
the Young Lion

Conrad felt no urge to run, or even to step back. He stood strong and steady, as if nailed into the path by his gleaming jackboots. The tank would stop. He would make it stop.

And it did stop. The heat and stench of the engine were overpowering, but Conrad could cope. It was towering over him, but he had made it stop and stand shuddering six feet away from him. Conrad was in control. He stood and waited, cool and steady, until another figure, an officer in a uniform like Conrad's own, emerged from the turret. Conrad's arm, as if moved by a mysterious force of his own, shot up above his head, and he watched as if in a dream as the other officer did the same and shouted: "Heil Hitler!"

Then, with a slow languid grace, the tank officer swung himself down from the turret and walked over to Conrad. He was tall and thin, with neat fair hair, and had a faint teasing smile that reminded Conrad of Ian Rowley, the most popular boy in his school, who monotonously won every race and captained every team, and charmed even Parkin with his manly ways. Now he stood in front of Conrad, relaxed and alert, the teasing smile just visible at the corners of his mouth.

"How's it going, Conrad?" he said.

Conrad stared at him open-mouthed. How did he know his name? Had he had instructions from Colditz to search him out and bring him back, had he recognized him from a photograph? There seemed to be more to it than that; this Rowley-like officer really seemed to *know* him.

Conrad stood and stared and awaited his fate.

And suddenly the teasing smile disappeared, to be replaced by a look of respect.

"But I forget myself," said the Rowley-like officer. He drew himself up to attention, and his boot heels clacked together. "Tank-Kapitan Johann von Rollereihen, reporting for duty as ordered," he said in clipped tones.

Then the smile again. "If we are to observe the formalities," he added, "I must ask to see your papers, Kolonel."

Conrad had a moment of panic. Papers? Papers? What papers? He was just a little boy. But his boots were tight and comforting around his calves, the eagles gleamed on his epaulettes, and he found himself reaching into an inside pocket he didn't know was there, and felt his fingers closing on the stiff square shape of an identity card. He took a quick glance at it before handing it to Rollereihen: KOLONEL KONRAD VON PIKEHOFEN.

The young German officer took it and handed it back. "Thank you, Kolonel," he said.

Conrad took a deep breath. "As your superior officer," he said, "I request that you hand over command of this tank to me." There was a second's silence that seemed like an hour to Conrad.

Then the charming smile again. "But of course, Kolonel," said Rollereihen. "Allow me to give you a leg up."

"What's our mission, then?" shouted Conrad over the roar of the engines, as the tank thundered over the rough country at a speed no English tank could match.

"The Kolonel knows as well as I do," smiled Rollereihen. "Simple stuff. Mopping up the pockets of resistance. They hide out in the outlying farmhouses around here. Helping prisoners, bombing bridges. We flush them out and shoot them. We don't take prisoners. When in doubt, blast them out."

He shrugged. "It's not work for heroes, Kolonel. But we have our duty to the Fatherland."

The Fatherland.

The *Fatherland?*

Was Conrad German now, then? Was he Konrad, now, Konrad the Young Lion? He tried very hard to hold his brains together in his head as he stared through the narrow slit at the grass and trees tossing and lurching in front of him. He felt strong in his German uniform, strong and strange and fierce. In a way it was something he had always wanted, war and violence, invincible at the controls of the most powerful tank in the world, blasting down buildings and crushing the opposition. He was the boss of everything now, in his German jackboots, with his German second-in-command smiling his German smile beside him, his German crew singing their German songs and telling their German jokes, ready to spring into action at his command. Together in their great Tiger monster-tank they could roll over the whole world, crush it out of existence beneath its tracks; win the war.

And it felt terrible. It was mixing his brains up so that he couldn't think. It was terrible to want two opposite things at once, to feel himself two different people. He (and who was he now? Conrad or Konrad?) felt that if he didn't get his brains under control he might lose himself forever, leak into a different person, a different past, a different world.

Sky, trees, road, grass, walls. They spun in front of him. He had to get his brains in order.

Rollereihen was saying something to him.

"What?" said Conrad/Konrad.

"I was saying, sir," said the smiling German, "couldn't we be Konrad and Johann, not Kolonel and Kapitan? After all, we were at school together; old school days never disappear entirely."

At school together? What did he mean? Was he Ian Rowley, then? Had he suffered under Parkin and the deadly long division? Or did he mean something else? As he stared through the slit, Konrad/Conrad suddenly saw a vision of different school days, some sort of military academy—standing in a long line at roll call in a tight, stiff uniform, a man with a waxed moustache bellowing orders, vaulting over a stained brown leather vaulting horse, a gymnasium where tough big boys in white suits slashed at each other with swords, some sort of outdoor cafe with a whole gang of boys in uniform singing and swaying and drinking from china mugs with lids on them.

Konrad and Johann. His brains were going. He had to do something. He had to get back into himself. He screwed his eyes tight shut, and concentrated desperately. Nothing. He tried again.

Then, like a miracle, he saw an image of Florence, standing in the door of her bedroom, holding a Womble under one arm and a teddy bear under the other.

"This Womble's been sick, Conrad," she said. "I'm taking him to the doctor's."

He opened his eyes. It was all right. His brains were straight again. He was Conrad, he was Conrad Pike and nobody else, and he was going to leak back out of this war and everything was going to be all right.

"School days?" he said to the German stranger beside him. "I was never at school with you, so you might as well shut up about it!"

And the teasing smile disappeared for good.

There was a shout from the turret above them. Conrad looked through the slit. Ahead of them on the road was a battered brown bus, with black and blue smoke puffing from its exhaust.

"The ambulance," said Rollereihen. "Do I give the order to open fire, Kolonel?"

"On an ambulance?" said Conrad. "Are you crazy?"

"The Kolonel knows very well that these accursed Resistance fighters use the ambulance as a cover for their movements. We have authority to fire from the Führer himself."

"Well, we're not going to and that's that," said Conrad.

"I'm in command here, Wiseguy, not you! Overtake it and stop. I'm going to have a look." The tank thundered past the laboring bus and stopped in its path. Conrad saw brown shadowy forms inside.

"Stay here," he said to Rollereihen.

"But it will be a trap! You'll be shot!"

"Oh, dry up," said Conrad. "Nobody's going to shoot me."

Conrad jumped down from the turret and walked back along the road to the bus. Everything had become very quiet. He could see no movement from inside the bus; the windows were very dirty, and inside, the shapes were dull and murky, like a neglected fish tank. Nobody opened the door for him, and he felt a strange reluctance to do it himself.

But he couldn't go back. It was all part of the war, and he had to get through it if he wanted to get out to the other side. He made himself walk to the door, slowly, left foot right foot, climb on the step, and swing the door open.

At first he couldn't see anything after the bright sunlight. Then things began to take shape. There were no proper seats in the bus; he couldn't even see one for the driver. There were just these long benches, covered with dirty brown blankets, and on the benches, humped in rows, were the shapes of wounded and dead people, men, women, and children. Everything was very quiet and still. There were no jerks and spasms like the dying in the army games at school, no screams or groans. Even the bloodstains looked old and brown.

Conrad started to feel himself going weak and small, and he felt a bit sick. He wished someone would move or speak or do something to show they were alive. It couldn't have been worse if it *had* been a trap, as Rollereihen had thought, and Resistance men had leaped out with guns from under the dirty brown blankets. But it wasn't a trap. Not that sort of trap. It was a trap for his feelings. This was the war the way his mother talked about it; her war had leaked into his war, sad and serious, and if something didn't happen very soon he was going to start crying.

Then a woman straightened up at the back of the bus from where she had been leaning over one of the huddled shapes. She stared at Conrad, quite unafraid of his Nazi uniform. She was a tall, skinny woman as old as his mother—older—but somehow she reminded Conrad of his sister Florence.

"What do you want?" she said. "Are you going to shoot us?"

"No," said Conrad. He heard his voice going all high and trembly. "I thought . . . is there anything we can do to help?"

The woman stared at him. "Have you got any medicine? Blood for blood transfusions? Have you got penicillin and dressings?"

"No," said Conrad helplessly. "We're a tank. We've just got things for killing people."

"Well," she said. "If you're not going to kill us, and you want to help us, maybe you'd better get your tank out of the road."

He looked at her and she stared back at him. He wanted to say something to help, but there was nothing to say.

He walked back to the tank and climbed back up.

"Get the tank off the road," he said to Rollereihen. The German stared at him but obeyed without comment.

Conrad waited until the sad brown bus had started up, passed them, and trundled away into the distance, leaving a trail of acrid fumes behind it. Then he turned to his men.

"Get out of the tank and stand by the side of the road," he said.

They stared at him.

"Go on," he said. "You heard. Get out of the tank."

The men got out. Rollereihen, biting his lip, stayed where he was. "Kolonel," he said hesitantly. "If it's about the orders to fire on the bus, I can assure you that I was merely following . . ."

Conrad didn't want to listen to him. "Go on, get down with the others!"

"But, Konrad, you were my best friend!"

"Get out of my tank!" yelled Conrad. Rollereihen got out of his tank.

Conrad started up, and wheeled the tank around until it was directly facing the line of Germans. They stood in a docile row, staring up at him, shielding their eyes against the bright sunlight. They didn't try to fight. They didn't try to run away. They just stood there waiting. They would stand there patiently, he knew, as he eased the tank forward over them and crushed them into the soft earth.

Conrad couldn't do it. He didn't want to kill the Germans. Standing down there they looked small and tired and frightened. Even Rollereihen, his teasing smile gone, looked like a tall, thin boy frightened of the dark. Everyone was frightened of something. And now they were all frightened of Conrad, and Conrad discovered that he didn't want it anymore.

He revved up the engine, saw Rollereihen fall on his knees, then abruptly pulled the tank around off the road and headed away to the right. Looking back minutes later, he could still see the little group by the side of the road, staring after him.

The Farm

The ground had been bucking and wheeling in front of him for what seemed like hours now, but he kept going, staring through the slit, as earth replaced road, and fields and hedges replaced earth. He was very tired now, but he knew he must be near; he had to keep going. The tank would go through almost anything, and Conrad was too tired to steer a careful route along smooth ground. He crashed the Tiger through fences and hedges, down steep banks into streams, water splashing up over the turret, gobs of mud flying off the tracks. On and on, the steel floor jolting under his feet, the engine roaring in his ears.

The sun had nearly gone down when he saw it. A low, gray, stone farmhouse clinging to the hillside. He eased back the throttle and the tank clawed its way up the hillside like a giant exhausted hedgehog. He had found the farm. He was going to be all right.

He stopped thirty yards from the farm and turned off the engine. The silence was so sudden and strong it was like a sound in itself. He could smell the grass. He could hear the birds singing. No more wars, no more Germans. It smelled like picnics.

He waited for a few more seconds in the tank, enjoying the silence and the fresh air and the feeling that he'd made it.

"I've done it," he said to himself. "I've found it all on my own." But the moment he said it he started to worry. Why weren't they coming out of the farmhouse to meet him? Surely they hadn't gone to bed yet? Conrad knew that in the country they went to bed early and got up early, but this was ridiculous. Resistance men should always be on the alert. He decided to get up on the turret and give them a shout.

He adjusted the peak of his cap to a smart and jaunty angle and stood up in the turret. Immediately he heard the splintering of glass, and almost simultaneously the crack of a rifle and the whine of a bullet going over his head. Conrad shot down again and found he was shaking.

What had happened? The worst thing of all? Had the Germans gotten there first? Had they taken over the farm and were they just sitting there waiting for him to turn up? What had they done with his dad? Rollereihen had said they weren't taking any prisoners. They couldn't have killed his dad. They couldn't have. He got up again.

"What have you done with my . . ." he started to shout, but another bullet whizzed over his head. He got down again quick. Lucky the Jerries were such rotten shots anyway.

Conrad peered out of the slit. Someone was crouching behind the low stone wall outside the farmhouse. The figure suddenly stood up and lobbed something in Conrad's direction. It landed right in front of the tank. A grenade! Conrad ducked and a second later there was a flash and a bang. That was all. The Tiger didn't even shake. Grenades. They could do a lot of harm to an armored car, but they were like firecrackers against a Tiger tank. Conrad suddenly realized that the Jerries wouldn't have expected him to turn up in a tank. He had the advantage in weaponry. He had them where he wanted them.

Slowly and deliberately he moved behind the controls of the great gun. Just a couple of shells would blast them out of existence. All he had to do was press the button. Conrad at the controls. They might have gotten his dad, but he'd show them. He moved his finger to the button.

Conrad couldn't do it. He didn't want to blast them out of existence at all. If they'd gotten his dad, then that was the end of it. He had seen the ambulance; he had let Rollereihen and his men go free; he had finished with killing now.

He let go of the button and slowly took the silly German hat off. Then he took the tight tunic off and felt the cool breeze blowing around him. Then he took the shirt off and waved it in the air above the turret.

"Don't shoot!" he called in a high, trembly voice. "I'm coming out."

He climbed unsteadily down from the tank and walked toward the farm. It seemed an amazingly long way and his legs felt wobbly and strange. Then he saw people coming out of the farm. People with guns.

The people weren't Germans. There were two short fat men with brown faces and moustaches, like farmers on Happy Families cards. They were grinning. The third man was his dad. Of course. *They* had thought *he* was the Jerry.

His head began to spin. There was a lot of talking and shouting in French and English, and they were half carrying him into the farmhouse, and he was half laughing and half crying and not able to say the things he wanted to say, and inside the farmhouse it was cool and dim, and there was a big scrubbed wooden table and barrels and jars, and a dog got up off the cool stone floor and came wagging toward him, and the dog looked like . . .

And the dog *was* . . .

Towzer!

Then he was sitting at the table and eating something out of a bowl, onion soup with bread in it, and Towzer's head was resting on his knee, and the spoon was getting heavier and heavier, and he couldn't hold his head up any longer, and his dad was carrying him up stone steps, and out of the corner of his eye he could see Towzer padding up the stone steps after him, and then he was sinking deep into a safe, soft feather mattress, and he was trying to tell them that he didn't really feel sleepy, and they were all smiling at him, then he was falling into a deep, dreamless sleep.

In the morning after he'd eaten six croissants and drunk three bowls of milky coffee they told him how Towzer had turned up at the farm three weeks ago, taking over the kitchen corner and barking for his dinner as if he owned the place. They had thrown him out three times, but each time he had returned in the middle of the night, disturbing their sleep with his outraged protests, and in the end they had decided to make the best of a bad job.

Then they told him that yesterday a hot, fat, confused, English writer with Nazi trousers and his shirt hanging out had staggered up the garden path and fallen in the horse trough, and shown no inclination to climb out of the cool water. They hadn't been able to understand what he was talking about, but as people in that part of the country had a tradition of charity toward harmless lunatics, village idiots, and the like, they had let him lie where he was, and when he had shambled in at suppertime when the smell of soup wafted out to the yard, they had made a place for him at the table and treated him as a guest, especially since he seemed to get on so well with their new dog.

And now everything was explained, and the farmers knew that the unlikely pair were the escaped prisoners they had been expecting, and Conrad and his dad knew that these fat little farmers were really the French Resistance, and that that night they would make their way to the coast where a boat would be waiting, and that everything was going to work out okay.

The farmers treated Conrad oddly, half as a little boy, half as if he were a visitor from Mars. After the breakfast and the explanations, they ushered him shyly out into the garden and invited him to play with their children. The children were ordinary enough, but they seemed to Conrad like children in a textbook, like Janet and John or Dick and Jane. Jean-Jacques and Simone, they were, in point of fact, and they played a game like croquet, except that the balls were heavy iron things and the green was a bit of rough and dusty turf. Conrad watched politely and took a turn whenever he was invited, but it all seemed very strange to him. It was so long since he had tried playing a game, just for the fun of it. Still. Better than soccer.

That night he lay in bed with all his equipment ready beside him for the two A.M. start, going over everything to himself, trying to hold in his head everything he had been through since the night of the Nuremberg raid, and all the things that had to be done in the morning to get them to the coast and into the boat and home to England, but he couldn't hold his thoughts together, they were all running together in a jumble, and he was sinking deeper and deeper into the warm soft cuddle of the big featherbed.

The Red Mist

Everything had gone according to plan all day. Conrad had woken up in a daze, hoping he might be back in his own room, but he found himself still in the fat featherbed in the French farmhouse. Still in the war, and more and more now he wanted to leak back. But he knew now he wasn't going to be able to do something that easy. He wasn't going to be able to leak back; that way he couldn't be sure he'd stay. No, he was going to have to travel all the distance there was to travel; he was going to have to come right out of the other end of the war.

Still, he'd seen a lot of war now, and this seemed to be

the soft end of it, the featherbed end, with croissants in bed and his dog on the blankets. Then there had been a lot of handshakes and short speeches from the Happy Families farmers, and then the tank again, mile after mile of it, bumping and grinding and roaring and reeking.

Conrad didn't mind now. He was going home and nothing was going to stop him. He was going home with his dad and his dog, and the tank was like a picnic tank, loaded with long loaves of bread and big round cheeses and bottles of red wine, from which the fat writer swigged huge gulps as he told Conrad and Towzer about the great TV series he planned about the French Resistance.

Conrad let him chatter on; it didn't seem worth telling him that the series would be no good, it would finish up like all the rest, too much kissing and talking and a pretty near certainty of nurses with tears in their eyes: the great writer just couldn't leave them out of anything. Let him chatter, Conrad thought. It was nice to hear him talk.

They had avoided towns, villages, and checkpoints, and they had kept off the roads and crashed the Tiger through rough country. They hadn't seen a living thing unless you counted an occasional cow.

"Maybe you could write about cows in your next play," said Conrad as they roared past their second one. "Where this soppy young cow had been eating the wrong sort of grass and the head cow gets her into the office and makes her cry. Just your kind of thing."

"It's been done," said his dad. "But it's a nice idea. You'll make a series writer yet. Pass that other bottle, would you?"

On and on like that, Conrad and his dad and his Towzer in the picnic tank, on and on until the sun came up, and as they reached the brow of each hill it seemed that it must be the last and they must see the sea, but instead another hill, and then another, and another, until at last, when Conrad had just managed to stop himself thinking "This one's the last," suddenly they had reached it.

Below them lay the beach, with its rubble and its shelled concrete gun turrets, and its barbed wire, and the long sweep of pale sand with the calm sea gently nibbling away at its edges like a baby sucking on a biscuit.

The Channel.

And most important of all—the boat. A small, shabby, old, open motor boat, moored to a buoy only ten yards out from the shore.

Conrad switched off the engine. In the sudden silence they could hear the gentle lapping of the sea. The morning sun was dazzlingly bright on the pale sand, and a small gang of seagulls bobbed up and down on the water a few yards farther out than the boat. The tank had crushed the barbed wire flat. All they had to do was walk across the sand, wade out through the shallow water, start the engine, and chug home out of the war.

Conrad took his boots off and jumped down into the soft sand, feeling the grains running between his toes. Towzer jumped down too and ran around him in circles, sniffing and whining. The fat writer descended more slowly, a big bottle of wine in each hand and a big cheese under each arm, loaves sticking out from every pocket. He looked like a rumpled octopus.

"You can't take all that," Conrad said. "You've got enough to last us a week."

"Feel a bit hungry," said his dad, staggering slightly. "Anyway, waste not, want not, that's what I always say about wine and cheese."

Conrad glared at his dad.

"I can see you think I'm a bit tight, but I'm not," said the great writer. "I am however slightly mellow. Who's game for a trip around the bay?"

It was just like a seaside picnic, thought Conrad as they made their way over the beach. All it needed was his mom and Florence and a couple of Wombles. What a nice way to go out of the war.

They had nearly reached the edge of the water when they heard the shout and the crack of gunfire and the bullet whined over their heads. Conrad whirled around. Half a mile up the beach were the figures of two German guards running in their direction, but much nearer, and getting closer every second, was a huge gray Alsatian dog coming straight for them, wasting no breath on barking and growling, just running them down.

"Quick!" said the writer. "Into the boat!"

They splashed and crashed through the shallow water. Loaves were going everywhere. Conrad and his dad tumbled into the boat headfirst, his dad pulled viciously on the frayed rope, and the engine fired the first time.

"Dad. We haven't got Towzer!"

Conrad and his dad stared in horror. Towzer was standing on the edge of the water, legs stiff, hackles up, ignoring them completely. His lips were drawn back from his teeth and he was snarling defiance at the enormous Alsatian, which was running straight for him.

"Towzer!" screamed Conrad. "Into the boat!"

"Towzer!" roared his dad. "Come here at once, sir!"

Towzer didn't move. It was like a horrible dream. The bright sand. Towzer standing motionless. The Alsatian moving silent and smooth as a machine, the gap closing with terrible speed.

It never slowed down. It crashed into Towzer and

knocked him head over heels. Towzer screamed and jumped up again and faced the Alsatian as it turned. It leaped on him slavering, going for his throat. Two piercing yelps, then Towzer had wriggled free. He had had enough now; he headed for the boat with terrified eyes, blood pouring from a nick in one of his ears. But he had no chance of reaching it. Conrad watched in horror, feeling as though his whole body were dissolving into slush, as the Alsatian caught Towzer in the shallow water and jumped on his back. He couldn't watch. He couldn't watch the Alsatian kill his Towzer dog. He put his face in his hands. Suddenly he heard a terrible roar, and something crashed past him, nearly knocking him into the water. His dad was rushing straight at the two dogs as they thrashed about in the water, waving a bottle of wine and howling horrible swear words, some of which Conrad had never heard.

The Alsatian raised its head as the fat body crashed toward it, and took a heavy blow in the chops from the wine bottle. Towzer wriggled free as the Alsatian launched itself at his dad.

"GERRROUTOFHERE!!!!" yelled his dad, purple in the face. Conrad had never seen him so angry before.

The Alsatian faltered as it leaped, such was the force of the writer's yell, and Conrad's dad belted it on the other side of the chops with the wine. The Alsatian sank back on its haunches in the shallows, snarling in an indecisive sort of way.

"WAAAAAARRRRRRRGH!" roared Conrad's dad as he rushed the Alsatian. The Alsatian hesitated for a split second, then quickly turned and splashed its way onto the sand, snarling over its shoulder.

"I'll get you, trying to kill our Towzer!" shouted the writer, stumbling after it.

"Dad!" squealed Conrad, suddenly able to speak again. "Get in the boat!"

His dad turned and stared in a puzzled sort of way. Then he clambered back into the boat. He put the engine into gear and cast loose, and the boat chugged away from the shore as the rifle shots started to whistle overhead again.

Conrad felt too tired and drained to cope with anything as they lay in the bottom of the boat. He stared at his dad's face, which was gradually returning to its normal glassy stare.

His dad caught his eye. "Hope I didn't alarm you too much," he said. "I got the Red Mist."

Time started to behave in a very strange way after that. Conrad felt sleepy and weak and very glad to be looked after by his dad and his dog. The sun was hot and the boat bobbed up and down, and sometimes he was looking up at the sky, and sometimes he seemed to be in his bed at home. There didn't seem to be any way he could control all this, but it didn't seem to matter too much. He wasn't responsible anymore. It wasn't his job. Once or twice he tried to say something to his dad. He wanted to say something about war and killing and about how he had gotten tired of it, and about how it was very complicated because if it wasn't for the Red Mist, Towzer would have been killed, but whenever he tried, the words came out in a jumble, or faded away to the rhythm of the rocking boat. Once when he was trying to explain it, and failing, his dad said to him, "It's all right, Conrad, it's all over now. You've won the war."

That sounded all right, that did. And Conrad allowed himself to sink into a deep and dreamless sleep.

Ending

Conrad was awake. He was in his own room. Everything looked the same, but Conrad felt older. He got up and put his bathrobe on and looked in Florence's room.

Nothing.

He looked in his parents' room.

Nothing.

It must be late. Imagine all of them getting up without him. He was losing his grip.

He stumped downstairs, jarring his knees on every step, and walked into the kitchen. They were all having breakfast. He took his seat and helped himself to a giant's portion of Frosties.

His dad looked at him strangely. "I had another peculiar dream about you last night," he said.

"Oh yeah?" said Conrad distantly.

"Yeah," said his dad. "We were both in the war together."

Conrad paused before speaking. He wanted to have everybody's attention.

"As a matter of fact," he said, "I'm getting a bit tired of war and army and killing and all that."

"*Really?*" said his mother.

"*Really?*" squeaked Florence.

"Yes, really," said Conrad. How many times did he have to say it? "As a matter of fact, I think I'll pack it in, and take up electricity."

His mother and father stared at him in disbelief for a moment, then turned to each other and smiled. Tender, triumphant smiles. Their son had gotten through a Difficult Phase. They turned to Conrad and beamed the tender triumphant smiles at him.

It was horrible. Conrad couldn't stand it.

"Yes," he said. "Very interesting, electricity. What I'm planning to do is build an electric chair."